Just My Merry Luck

JAMIE LEE FRY

Just My Merry Luck

JAMIE LEE FRY

Print edition ISBN: 9798988215660
eBook edition ISBN: 9798988215677

First edition: November 2025
10 9 8 7 6 5 4 3 2 1

WWW.AUTHORJAMIELEEFRY.COM

For my favorite travel companion, Jeremy.
We will always have our perfect Paris day.

Chapter One

Every first of December, the tenth floor of Foster & Sons magically morphs into a winter wonderland, buzzing with the chatter of holiday plans, and decked out with more twinkling lights than one small space should ever incur—this year is no different from the last four.

I have a sneaking suspicion that Bevin from accounting, with her annoyingly festive sweaters, is the little elf behind this year's decorating extravaganza. But keeping with the holiday magic of it all, she'll never take credit. It's all very festive and cute, albeit a bit distracting.

I mean, this is an office after all.

I'm not a Grinch or anything; I just don't prioritize the holidays like my co-workers do. I have my reasons. Plus, I'm too busy—a self-proclaimed workaholic. That's why I skillfully avoided the sign-up sheet for today's festive-themed potluck. But let's be honest: no one is missing the sad, store-bought cupcakes I would have brought.

I grit my teeth as another rendition of "It's the Most

Wonderful Time of the Year" hums through the speakers. I swear this is the third version I've heard today, and it's not even noon.

This is going to be the longest month ever.

It doesn't help that I'm on a ridiculously tight deadline. Year-end projects have been stacking up on my desk—all courtesy of my incredibly inefficient coworkers.

Talk about waiting until the last minute, guys.

I can't do my work until they do theirs, and that simple fact irritates the merry little Christmas out of me. If it were up to me, I'd do it all myself. Unfortunately, that's not how things work around here. But if I can power through this next stack of advertising comparison reports—*sounds fun, doesn't it?*—then maybe I can sneak off for one of those delicious-looking cookies from the overly decorated table behind me. Like I said, I'm not a Grinch—I love a well-decorated cookie. I'm just not baking my own these days.

As thoughts of sweet treats and comp reports flicker through my mind like the distracting twinkling lights through the office, a paperclip flies past my head, landing with a clatter on my desk.

"Earth to Jemma!" Gretchen's voice slices through the stale office air, her words competing with the holiday tune streaming from the speakers.

Gretchen is my office bestie—okay, my only bestie—and quite possibly the most positive person I've ever met. Having been hired a whopping six months before me, she took me under her wing, and we've been connected at the hip ever since. We no longer work in the same department, but thankfully, our desks are still next to each other.

Gretchen is working her way up the marketing ladder, while I'm still stuck in advertising analysis. I love my job and I'm good at it, but I'd much rather be in marketing. That's one of the reasons I work so hard—*one of them.*

I lift my head to meet Gretchen's gaze, offering her a curious grin. "What?" I mouth.

Her large, expressive, amber-colored eyes light up as she nods toward the conference room. "They're calling you in," she whispers.

"Me?" I question, my eyebrows practically leaping off my forehead. That can't be right. I don't have anything on my calendar this afternoon. Gretchen must have misheard.

But being the nosy person I am, I stealthily roll my chair back behind the line of desks to see what's going on.

Okay, that's strange.

The conference room at the end of the hallway—the one that's only used when the bigwigs are in town—is filling up with board members, human resource staff, and a few people I don't recognize.

Seriously, how did I miss all the commotion?

Just as I squint to get a better look, one of the younger board members strides across the room and presses a button on the wall, transforming the transparent window into an opaque screen, obscuring my view inside.

Dang it.

"Jemma Jones," a husky voice barks, nearly knocking me off my office chair, ending my spy mission. A short woman with pinched features, balancing a stack of manila folders in her arms, appears in the conference room doorway.

"Jemma Jones," she repeats, this time louder.

I glance back at Gretchen, who offers me a hesitant smile, but quickly masks it with a reassuring flick of her wrist as if to say everything will be fine—nothing to worry about. *Queen of positivity, remember?* But they don't call you into *this* conference room without a scheduled meeting unless it's something to worry about. And this definitely feels like something to worry about.

Did I make a mistake or something? Are they calling me in to issue a formal write-up? But for what? I do a quick mental inventory of all the reports I sent last month, but nothing jumps out. Sure, I feel behind today, but that's because other people are lazy. Not me. I always get everything done on time, even if that means staying late. I've never made a big mistake. So, what could they possibly want with me?

I rise from my chair, my stomach in knots and grumbling from thoughts of uneaten Christmas cookies. I take a deep breath, pushing down the anxiety that's attacking my nerves, and march toward the conference room, sidestepping the table of festive snacks. My cheeks feel hot as the fluorescent lights overhead shine down on me like a spotlight.

Everyone's eyes are on me.

Great, just what I need—an audience.

I hesitantly enter the blindingly white conference room, my heart racing as I face the intimidating people in fancy suits seated around a long oak table. Their expressions are smug and uptight.

'Tis the season . . . to be grumpy, I suppose.

One of them gestures for me to take a seat. As I lower myself into the chair, my palms grow sweaty. I nervously play with the ends of my long, honey-blonde hair that's meticulously braided down the side of my neck and resting neatly against my white sweater as I wait for someone to speak.

Seriously, someone say something before I go crazy!

Everyone's heads turn toward the door as the Director of HR enters. He's tall and slender, with a receding hairline, and for the life of me I can't remember his name. Tom? Ted? Something with a T. Foster & Sons has over one thousand employees, yet oddly none of them are sons. It's hard for me to keep track of everyone, especially since most of the higher-ups dwell on the floor above mine and hardly make time for the little people, unless there's a problem.

The man, whose name is still evading me, positions himself in front of the table but doesn't sit. Instead, he takes a firm stance and stares straight ahead, looking past everyone. He adjusts his baby-blue tie while the entire room hangs in silence.

Get on with it, dude!

Finally, he turns to face me, his muddy brown eyes finding mine. "Ms. Jones," he begins.

My breath hitches in my throat.

"I'm so sorry, but we're letting you go."

Chapter Two

JEMMA

Time seems to freeze—*let me go?* I can hardly process what he's saying.

"But—I don't understand," I stammer. "Let me go?"

He narrows his gaze and exhales sharply. "The year-end adjustments have forced us to make some difficult decisions," he continues, his rehearsed tone piercing through my haze of confusion. "We're offering you a severance package and a Christmas bonus that's well padded. We know this isn't easy, and the timing is poor, being the start of the holiday season and all. The funds will be directly deposited into your bank account by the end of the business day. We just need your signature on a few forms here." He slides an open folder toward me, but I barely register the action.

I'm frozen in place, his words still ringing in my ear— *let me go.*

He gives me an encouraging nod to pick up the pen someone conveniently placed beside me. Still in shock, I take it and sign by all the X's. As my pen glides across the final line, I glance at the HR Director, and suddenly, it clicks—his name is Tyler. A flash of sympathy crosses Tyler's dull eyes, and for a fleeting second, I actually feel bad for the guy, having to deliver news like this right before the holidays. But then, like a sharp slap in the face, reality hits me: he doesn't care about me. His concern is wrapped up in budget sheets, bottom lines, and protocol. The bonus he's offering is nothing but a calculated attempt to avoid any backlash.

"Is it something I did?" I ask, shrinking into my chair.

Tyler's posture stiffens, and I notice he keeps glancing at someone at the other end of the table, but I don't allow myself to follow his gaze. "No, it's just that we need to make cuts, and you were the last one hired in your department."

"But how is that even possible? I've worked here for four years. Please," I plead, even though I know it's useless.

I've already foolishly signed the paperwork. Truth is, I was the last person hired, but I've surpassed my colleagues, which means I likely earn more than they do. This is probably why I'm being fired and not them. *Go figure.*

"Yes, but others have been here longer and bring more value to the company."

That's a bunch of bull.

"You do understand, right?" He nods, expecting me to join him in this twisted acceptance of corporate logic.

I remain still, even though my gut is telling me to stand up and fight—to give this man a piece of my mind —to tell him how incredibly unfair this is. He should know my department can't function without me. And the people who've been here longer are lazy. But the suits in the room are turning me into an insecure mess. I suppose that's the whole point of them being here, isn't it?

My shoulders sag, and an audible huff escapes my perfectly pink glossed lips.

"We have to protect marketing first and foremost. It's why we're here." His lips soften, and an infuriating grin plays at the corner of his mouth. "Your department isn't the only one seeing cuts," he reassures me, although it's doing nothing of the sort.

My thoughts gravitate to Anthony, an expensive new hire in sales and a proud new father to twins—will he be next? Dang, the corporate greed machine.

Nausea churns in my stomach, threatening to spill over onto the polished conference room table in front of me, a table that likely costs more than a month of my salary.

All the work I poured into this job—all the late nights and early mornings—only to have it culminate like this.

"That will be all, Ms. Jones." He gestures toward the door. "We do wish you a Merry Christmas."

"Thank you," I whisper, standing. My throat is tight as I nod, struggling to keep my composure.

Thank you?

Why on earth did I say that?

He just fired me.

My legs wobble as I walk out, tears brimming from my eyes. On autopilot, I swipe an obscene handful of cookies from the table—the very cookies I wished to enjoy just moments ago—and mope back to my desk, all eyes still on me.

I slide open the bottom drawer of my file cabinet and retrieve my purse, coat, and a reusable shopping bag I keep on hand for emergencies, quickly filling it with my belongings.

Well, I guess that's everything.

Gretchen watches me closely and follows me into the hallway. The instant the door swings shut behind us, I crumble. The floodgates burst open, and an uncontrollable sob takes over me.

"What the heck just happened?" she asks. "Why are you leaving?"

I shove a snowman-shaped cookie into my mouth, attempting to drown my sorrow in sweetness. Tears stream down my cheeks and into my mouth, mixing with the sugary bliss, turning it sour. "They let me go," I manage to choke out. "I think your job is safe," I add between bites, waving the snowman in Gretchen's face.

"I'm not worried about me right now, Jemma." She waits until I finish chewing, then pulls me into a tight hug, her thick, wild, caramel-colored hair wrapping around me like a comforting cape. "Ugh, this is so unfair! I can't believe they're doing this to you right before Christmas."

"I can," I sob.

Gretchen pulls back just enough to meet my gaze. She studies me with a familiar intensity, and I brace myself for one of her signature uplifting pep talks. It's what she's known for. Feeling sad? Go to Gretchen. Need a mood boost? Go to Gretchen. Sometimes I think she should write a self-help book.

"Jemma," she begins, wagging her finger at me. "You're not going to let this get you down. You got that?"

I can't seem to get my mouth to do anything but frown, so I force a nod to appease her.

"Now, hear me out," she insists. "This sucks. I'm mad for you. Like, seriously mad. This isn't cool. But what can you do about it?"

I crinkle my nose. "Where are you going with this, Gretch?"

"I said hear me out. So impatient." She smirks, tossing her thick hair over one shoulder. "You're a workaholic, Jemma. I know your goal was to move into marketing, but sometimes the universe has other plans for you. You were missing out on life, and for what?"

I huff, crossing my arms defensively. "I don't know, maybe to pay rent?"

Truth is, this layoff couldn't have come at a worse time. I need the distraction.

Gretchen rolls her eyes. "Okay, true. But there's more to life than just a job. Think of this as the universe showing you it's time to realign your priorities. You eat three meals a day at your desk. You haven't been on a date in God knows how long. When I met you, all you talked about was traveling and visiting places like Paris. What happened to that Jemma?"

That Jemma doesn't exist anymore.

"Find her," Gretchen says as if she's listening to my very thoughts. "Things like this don't happen without good reason." She gives my shoulder an encouraging pat. "Find the silver lining in all this. Do the things you've been putting off, like taking a trip somewhere—anywhere. I'm begging you to do something for yourself." She's practically shaking me.

"Traveling without a job isn't exactly smart, Gretchen," I protest, even as the thought of my well-padded Christmas bonus lingers enticingly in the back of my mind.

"Regardless," Gretchen says, pulling us back as the door swings open.

I hear voices, but I don't turn around. I don't want anyone to see me like this.

Gretchen shoos them away before continuing. "Take this well-deserved time off, and at least do me a favor and try to embrace the Christmas season. I can't help but feel like you've been avoiding it for the past few years, throwing yourself into work as an excuse. When was the last time you decorated your apartment or visited your dad for the holidays? And don't think I didn't notice you sneaking in today without a dish to pass out. This isn't the Jemma I first met. Find yourself again. Make the most of this time off, Jemma. This time is a gift."

"Some gift," I mutter.

But she's right about everything. However, the thought of spending Christmas with my dad feels far from enticing. Ever since he remarried just three short years after my mom's passing, everything feels complicated. He's completely wrapped up in his new family—my Step-Monster and her trio of little gremlins.

I appreciate Gretchen's attempt to make good of a bad

situation, but I truly don't know what I'm going to do now.

"Give some thought to what I said. You never know what amazing opportunities might be waiting for you. I have a good feeling about this, Jem. And you know I'm never wrong." She laughs, tossing her head back slightly.

Despite all my worries, a small smile spreads across my face. *The Gretchen effect.*

"I'll text you later," Gretchen adds. "Let's meet up for drinks, my treat. Okay?"

I nod.

"Now I'd better get back to work before I find myself on the chopping block too." She flashes me a playful wink. "We can't both lose our jobs today; one of us has to be able to buy those drinks." With that, she disappears through the door, leaving me alone with my thoughts.

I admire Gretchen's unwavering optimism; she has an uncanny ability to illuminate the darkest situations. I mean, I just got fired, and somehow, she has me believing this could be a good thing. I guess only time will tell.

I race down the ten flights of stairs, avoiding the elevator to steer clear of any chance encounters with my former co-workers. Before opening the double glass doors for the last time, I slip on my red trench coat, cinching it snugly around my waist, dreading the bitter cold that's bound to be waiting for me. But as I step outside, under the fancy awning and into the chaos of New York City, I'm unexpectedly greeted by a burst of warmth.

Okay, so maybe Gretchen is onto something here. I know it's just the weather, but perhaps this is the universe's way of showing me things are looking up, and better things are coming. Or maybe I just drank the Gretchen Kool-Aid.

As I pivot to walk away from the building that I'll probably never step foot inside again, I come across a man wearing a tattered Santa hat, shaking a sleigh bell, calling out for donations on the sidewalk. Usually, I would shuffle past, eyes glued to the pavement, but something stops me.

Feeling Gretchen's positivity clinging to me like a fresh coat of paint, I rummage through my purse, pull out a crinkled ten-dollar bill, and toss it into the shiny red donation tin.

The man looks up, beaming, with a twinkle in his eye. "Thank you for your kindness, miss. Merry Christmas."

"You're very welcome. Merry Christmas to you too," I reply, feeling a warmth stir in my belly.

"Everything always works out as it should. Let go and follow the signs."

"Excuse me?" I cock my head to the side, puzzled by his words, as if he knows what just happened in the building behind me.

But he's already turned his attention to the next kind New Yorker stuffing dollar bills into his red tin.

I shake my head, questioning my sanity. Either way, I hope everything does work out. But as I walk a few blocks, panic starts to creep back in. If I take a left and head toward the subway, I know what awaits me—pajamas, ordering in, sobbing for a few hours, and replaying every moment of the last four years in my head. No, I can't do that to myself.

Keep walking Jemma. Just go with the flow.

Well, the flow seems to be leading me toward Fifth Avenue. I don't fight it; I just go with it.

Big, soft snowflakes begin to flutter down as I stroll along Manhattan's most decorated street—a street I've strategically avoided the past few Decembers. But as I pass the glittering storefronts, each window beautifully decorated for the holidays, one display catches my attention, stopping me dead in my tracks. Tears immediately spring to my eyes.

If this isn't a sign, I don't know what is.

Amidst the shimmering decorations, a mini snow-dusted Eiffel Tower stands majestically, surrounded by delicate, glistening snowflakes. A flood of tears stream down my cheeks, racing to my chin, chilling my skin.

I miss the old me.

I miss the me that planned to visit Paris one day.

I miss the me that enjoyed Christmas.

Gretchen is right; I need to find her.

I let my imagination run wild as visions of Christmas in Paris swirl through my mind, stirring my soul. I can almost picture the twinkling lights adorning the Champs-Élysées and the scent of fresh buttery pastries wafting through the crisp winter air.

If I stay here and find another job, I know I'll sink back into old habits. There's a reason I became a workaholic and turned my back on Christmas. Happiness feels like a stranger now. But that ends today.

I press my hand against the cold window, feeling the coolness seep into my skin, grounding me in this moment of clarity.

Paris, here I come.

Chapter Three

JEMMA

It turns out that deciding to fly to Paris on a whim isn't as romantic as it sounds. Especially at Christmastime. I'm striking out left and right with each airline as the vision of sipping on iconic chocolat chaud in a Parisian café dims along with it. Prices are insane, and choices are limited.

I take a heavy sip from the wine I poured hours ago, my only companion in this frustrating quest, and switch from airline websites to travel apps, desperately hoping for a last-minute miracle. I could wait a few days or months, but I know myself. I'll back out. I'll find a reason not to go.

I add my search: New York (JFK) to Paris (Charles de Gaulle)—December 4 to December 26—one traveler. I take a deep breath, bracing myself for an inevitable letdown.

The screen lights up with a single, staggering result—one flight left in Premium Economy for $1,832.

Ouch.

I hesitate, finger hovering over the "Book Now" button.

It's now or never, Jemma.

Just as I feel my courage build, I nervously pull up my bank account to confirm my former employer paid me. Tyler assured me that the money would arrive by the end of the day. Sure enough, my severance and Christmas bonus are in my account as promised. It's more than I assumed it would be. But this ticket would completely obliterate my bonus.

What if I don't get a job when I return? I'll be left with hardly any safety cushion. But on the other hand, I can't sit around here and stew all month, applying for jobs from my lumpy couch. I can just as easily apply for openings in a Parisian café while sipping on an espresso and delighting in a buttery, flaky croissant. Yes, that sounds much better.

With a deep sigh and a swig of my wine, I click buy.

The screen flashes an error message—SOLD OUT.

You've got to be kidding me.

I hit refresh, hoping against hope.

It reloads, and just like that, the flight is back.

I let out a sigh and snatch the opportunity, clicking through the prompts before I can second-guess my possibly irresponsible decision yet again.

A text from Gretchen buzzes on my phone just as I confirm my booking. I'm dying to tell her about my insanely impulsive plans. She'll be so proud of me. After all, I wouldn't have had this idea without her pushing me.

Gretchen: Whimsies at 9 p.m.? Care if
Suzy tags along?

Seriously, Gretch?

How many times do I have to tell her that her girlfriend is always welcome? I adore Suzy. Plus, after two years of dating, it's kind of assumed she's coming. I'd expect the same if I ever found someone. Although I can't help but feel a twinge of envy when I think of them. Gretchen and Suzy are so perfectly matched in that opposites attract kind of way. It's been ages since I've had something like that. That whole being a workaholic thing. I've completely wasted my twenties. And for what?

Staring down at my phone, I quickly tap out a response before I accidentally fall back into old habits and pull up Google to start job hunting. Typical Type A personality here. The urge is strong, but it's time to live in the moment. *Let go.*

Jemma: I'll be there, and Suzy is always
welcome. You never have to ask. STOP
ASKING!!!

I decide not to spill the beans about my trip just yet. I still need to find a hotel before I get too confident in this totally out of character idea. My phone illuminates in my hand with a response.

Gretchen: You're the best!!!! See you
soon! Remember, all the drinks you can
consume tonight are on me! 😜

I glance at the clock on my phone, realizing that gives me only an hour to find a hotel. I crack my knuckles and return to my keyboard, determined to hunt for a place to stay. But it seems finding a hotel is almost harder than landing the flight, so I switch my tactics yet again, moving to a vacation rental site.

As I scroll through the options, one apartment catches my eye—so perfect and charming it almost feels too good to be true. It's a sun-drenched loft nestled in the heart of the Marais, complete with large, arched windows that lead out to a small balcony overlooking a cozy café. The view from the bedroom is even more stunning, as it offers a breathtaking sight of a picturesque cobblestone courtyard brimming with potted greenery and cute little wooden benches.

I quickly scan the rest of the details. It's in my budget, well-reviewed, and the host sounds welcoming. This is the sort of place where I can reset and figure out my next move. It's perfect.

This time, I don't hesitate. I click "Reserve Now" and send my deposit without a second thought.

I lean back in my chair, feeling excited for the first time in a very long time.

I'm really doing this.

I'm going to Paris.

Chapter Four

JEMMA

I immediately catch sight of Gretchen and Suzy at their usual booth. Suzy's hair is always an adventure, keeping in line with her unpredictable personality. Tonight, her new short pixie cut with soft pink highlights practically beams under the bar lights, making the pair hard to miss.

"Jemma! You made it!" Gretchen exclaims, leaping up to envelop me in one of her signature bear hugs. "Again, I'm so sorry about this morning." She immediately hands me a glass of red wine. "Got your usual."

"Thanks." I say, reaching for the stem.

"I'm sorry too, Jemma. What a total crock of crap," Suzy adds, taking a leisurely sip of her whisky, not bothering to get up.

I love Suzy's blunt, no-nonsense approach to everything. There's no beating around the bush with her. She's always straightforward, and tonight is no exception.

"Total crock of crap," I agree, taking a large gulp of the

earthy, full-bodied wine, letting the bitterness rest on my tastebuds.

"And what a cruddy time to let staff go—during a holiday potluck—what a bunch of Scrooges." Suzy huffs, twisting her tiny features upward in disgust.

Gretchen slides into the booth, curling up next to her girlfriend.

I take my spot, settling in across the table from the cute duo. "It's OK. I'll be just fine," I mutter unconvincingly. "I'm glad you still have a job, though." I nod to Gretchen. "Who else got let go after me this morning? Please tell me it wasn't Anthony."

My stomach drops waiting for her response.

She pulls in a deep breath. "Yes, Anthony and Sally Hemsworth from Sales. Oh, and that new guy Bill from Creative. Plus, a bunch of people from the ninth floor and all the temp hires. You're lucky you were one of the first. Everyone was on pins and needles all day. It was so awkward." Gretchen frowns, then her eyes shift, practically lighting up. "But let's not dwell on sadness tonight. Perhaps this is the fresh start everyone needs. Maybe Anthony can finally be the stay-at-home dad he's always dreamed of being. And Sally—this could be the push she needs to start that jewelry line she won't stop talking about. As for Bill . . . Well, who knows what he'll do, but maybe he'll discover something amazing. And you, my dear friend—"

"I—I," I stutter, cutting her off. "I actually have some big news," I say, leaning in slightly, locking eyes with my friends.

"Spill it!" Gretchen urges, a curious twinkle flashing in her golden eyes.

I bite my bottom lip, nervous to spill the beans because that means it's real, but the words just tumble out. "I'm going to Paris!"

Suzy's jaw drops, and Gretchen claps her hands together, practically bouncing in her seat.

"That's freaking amazing! I'm so glad you're doing something for yourself for once. I see my pep talk worked this morning." Gretchen beams proudly.

"You're pretty convincing when you want to be," I respond, running a finger along the rim of my glass.

"So, when do you leave?" Gretchen presses.

"Thursday night," I say, feeling the gravity and the excitement of my impulsive decision settle in. "I booked my flight and an amazing vacation rental in the Marais. Am I crazy? I lost my job this morning, and now I'm taking the trip of a lifetime to Paris, of all places."

"Crazy? No way! This is epic! You deserve every bit of this." Gretchen lifts her glass high. "To new adventures and fresh starts. You deserve this, Jemma."

I raise my glass to clink with hers.

"Speaking of adventures, can I ask you a favor?"

"Anything," she replies without hesitation.

I know what I'm about to ask isn't exactly a fun favor, but it's an adventure of sorts. "Can you give me a ride to JFK on Thursday night? I booked the red-eye flight. I'd owe you big time. Please. Please," I beg.

Gretchen takes a dramatic sip from her expensive cocktail. "For you, I'd drive to the ends of the earth, darling."

She chuckles. "But seriously, yes. That way, I can keep an eye on you and make sure you don't chicken out." She winks. "Oh, but I'll have to take Suzy's car; mine's on the fritz again."

"You're the best—both of you. Thank you."

"Don't you mean merci? You do know some French, right?" Suzy asks in her dry, teasing tone.

I flash her a confident smile. "Je parle un peu français. I took four years of it in college. I was good at it. Not fluent by any means, but I could hold a conversation pretty well."

"Sweetie, that was eight years ago," Gretchen kindly reminds me, raising a skeptical eyebrow.

Eight years ago—the thought gnaws at my insides. It's been eight years since college. Two back-to-back corporate jobs devoured my free time in the name of security and money, only for it all to unravel.

Nope, I'm not going to think about that now.

"I hope you've managed to stash a bit more French in your brain since then," Suzy adds.

With a playful smirk, I quip, "J'adore—" The French word for wine evades my memory.

My friends patiently wait for me to get it.

"Ah yes, j'adore le vin rouge. See? It will come back to me."

"Slowly." Suzy chuckles.

"Wow, I'm leaving for Paris in seventy-two hours!" I exclaim. "And I still need to pack. I have no idea what I'm getting myself into, do I?"

"Girl, please tell me you have your passport, right?" Gretchen asks, leaning in.

"Yes, Mother." I giggle. "I know this is last minute, but I'm not one-hundred percent unprepared. I always keep my passport up to date—you know—just in case. But the real question we need to be asking is, what the hell am I going to pack?"

"Oh-oh!" Gretchen taps her hand excitedly against the table. "You have to take my red long-sleeved dress—the one you gushed about last Christmas! I'll drop it off first thing tomorrow morning. Trust me, you'll look stunning in it. And who knows? Maybe you'll even catch the eye of a hot Frenchman while you're at it." She suggestively wags her eyebrows at me.

"Maybe," I say, my cheeks warming at the idea.

Gretchen tilts her head to the side. "See, sometimes the universe knows what it's doing. I know things were gloom and doom this morning, but heck, Jem, look at you now. You're going to Paris. You wouldn't have taken this leap if you hadn't been fired this morning. You'd still be saying someday. But that someday is in three days."

I tuck a loose strand of my braid behind my ear. "I suppose you're right. Sure, I still need to do some major job hunting while I'm away, but I should take this time to enjoy myself too. Right?"

"Exactly! I was expecting a sulking fest tonight, but look at us—we're here to celebrate!" Gretchen smiles and slides out of the booth.

Suzy follows.

"Let's make tonight unforgettable, shall we?" Gretchen lends me a hand and tugs me toward the dance floor.

"Let's," I respond, ready to embrace my new adventure

—or should I say, Je suis prête à embrasser ma nouvelle aventure.

Chapter Five

JEMMA

Thursday evening creeps up faster than I expected. I double and triple-check my quick packing job, ensuring I've got all my essentials: my passport, a few carefully chosen outfits that I can mix and match to save space, and, of course, Gretchen's red dress that I can't wait to wear. She was right; it does look great on me.

Look out, Paris, here I come!

Gretchen pulls up outside my apartment in Suzy's little blue Volkswagen Bug. Its paint is slightly more rusted than I remember, but it has a lot of character, just like Suzy. Gretchen's ride isn't much nicer—just less rust and barely hanging on for dear life. But really, who needs a car in the city? Public transportation works just fine. Well, except when you're hauling a bunch of luggage to the airport, and you want your best friend by your side until the very last minute, so you don't chicken out. Or maybe that's just me.

"Where's Suzy?" I ask, shoving my suitcase and carry-on into the tiny back seat. "I thought maybe she'd come keep you company for the late drive home."

"Nah, work emergency. A crazy huge order was placed last minute for an early pickup tomorrow, and the staff couldn't handle it. So, Suzy to the rescue, as usual." Gretchen tosses her hand in the air as she checks her mirror, pulling into traffic.

Suzy is a pastry chef at one of the cutest little bakeries down the street from Whimsies. Just thinking of the place makes my mouth water. But then I quickly remember that in less than a day I'll be in a city known for having some of the best pastries in the world. I close my eyes, envisioning myself biting into a buttery croissant, the flaky layers melting in my mouth. I'm lost in buttery bliss, when suddenly my body pitches forward as Gretchen slams on the brakes, yanking me away from my delicious daydream.

My eyes whip open to a gridlocked expressway.

Great. Just what we need.

Thanks to Suzy's tiny car, Gretchen does a good job inching into a lane, but we're barely crawling forward, and the minutes are ticking away. I can already picture myself stuck behind a long line at check-in and missing my flight. This can't be happening.

I keep glancing at the clock, silently pleading with the traffic to part.

My heart plunges into my stomach.

"Maybe this flight wasn't meant to be," I whisper. "Maybe this is a sign."

"Oh, heck no. I'm getting you to that airport," Gretchen declares, slamming down on the horn.

She expertly weaves through a sea of SUVs and semi-trucks. One moment we're parting two lanes, and the next, she's trucking down the gravelly shoulder. This must be what it's like driving an emergency vehicle. Part of me is hanging on for dear life, while the other part is grinning like a lunatic.

We might make it after all.

Gretchen is completely unfazed by the whirlwind of chaos she's creating. We speed past an elderly woman who can barely see over the steering wheel; her face contorts with disdain as she raises her middle finger at us.

"I think you're making some new friends!" I joke.

"If they only knew the stakes here, they would totally understand," she replies with such conviction that it makes me think she truly believes that.

However, I'll never give people that kind of credit—especially New Yorkers. Out here, it's every person for themselves.

Without missing a beat, she rolls down her window and shouts, "Merry Christmas!" while waving energetically.

I can't help but burst into laughter. I love this girl! I'm so grateful we met at Foster & Sons, even if they did kick me to the curb just days ago.

Finally, the traffic eases up, and we hit a steady pace. With a victorious grin, Gretchen cranks up the music, turning the car into our own little version of carpool karaoke. I use everything I can find as a microphone—a phone, my hand, a pen—belting out every song that plays. It's a fun distraction, but I keep my eyes fixed on the clock ticking away.

When we take the airport exit, I feel a wave of relief, but I know I still need everything to align perfectly to make it on time.

"Thanks again for the ride. I'm pretty darn impressed with your mad racecar skills. I don't think an Uber driver or a cabbie could have pulled off what you did back there. I'm so glad I asked you," I say as the car comes to a screeching halt in front of a busy terminal.

Gretchen whirls around in her seat and dramatically grabs my hands. I swear I can feel her energy vibrating between us. "Jemma, I wish you the most magical Christmas of your life. Don't overthink things, and most importantly, have fun." Her words tumble out in a quick, jumbled string.

"You're so dramatic, but seriously, thank you." I swing my door open and begin to wrestle my luggage from the back seat. "I'll text you once I settle in. I hope you and Suzy have a wonderful Christmas too. May Santa bring you everything you wish for—maybe even an engagement ring," I tease, flashing her my ring finger.

A slow smile spreads across my friend's face, and with that, I whip around, quickly locating the closest entryway.

"Don't forget to buy a SIM card at the airport!" Gretchen calls after me, her voice cutting through the sound of cab drivers impatiently honking their horns.

Cell service.

Her words nearly knock the wind out of me. How could I have forgotten to consider how my phone will work once I'm there? Thank goodness for Gretchen—the world's best friend—always looking out for me. What would I do without her? I should have made a to-do list or did a bit more research, but there's no time to overthink things now. I've got a plane to catch.

I burst through the revolving doors, my eyes darting to the overhead signs pointing me toward my airline's counter.

Alright, Jemma, you can freaking do this.

I might need a small miracle, but I'll make this flight.

I dash through the airport, my suitcase bouncing behind me as I race to the check-in counter. Thankfully, the line is short. Once it's my turn, I hurl my luggage onto the scale and proceed with all the necessary steps to finally get my coveted ticket to Paris.

Next, I make a beeline for TSA, where the security line feels like an Olympic event—shoes off, laptop out, arms raised for the invasive body scanner.

Ugh. I always hate this part.

I clumsily gather my belongings, slipping back into my shoes as I juggle my boarding pass, random receipts from dropping off my luggage, and my passport. Then, I sprint toward my gate on the other side of the airport.

I'm panting and nearly out of breath as I keep checking the signs above me, making sure I'm heading in the right direction. I'm searching for Gate B52, but I'm only at B19. I better pick up my pace, or I'm not going to make it.

I look up again, noticing I need to take a left. As I pivot to turn down the long corridor, out of the corner of my eye, I see a tall guy decked out in what can only be described as an elf costume—green tunic, pointed hat, the whole nine yards—racing toward me.

I hardly have time to react. Just as I swing to avoid colliding with him, I swear I see a twinkle in his eye, and then *bam*—I crash right into another man instead. Our plane tickets and papers fly across the busy terminal floor, scattering like confetti.

"Eh. Watch where you're going!" the man snaps, his accent thick and sharp.

I'm utterly mortified.

Avoiding eye contact, we both crouch down to gather the scattered papers. As I reach for the last item, fate deals me another blow. We bump heads, adding a fresh layer of embarrassment to an already awkward situation. I want the floor to open up and swallow me whole.

When I finally muster the courage to stand, I find him scowling at me with the bluest eyes I've ever seen. Seriously, dude, are those contact lenses? No one has eyes that frosty blue.

His irrefutable handsomeness momentarily makes my breath hitch.

"I—I'm so sorry," I stutter, struggling to tear my gaze away from the gorgeous creature whose dark brown hair is falling in waves, tousled in that sexy, effortless kind of way. The kind that makes you want to reach out and rake your fingers through it. But, of course, I fight the urge, because that would be weird, right? His strong jaw is freshly shaven, yet tightly clenched, presumably out of irritation with me for crashing into him. My eyes drift downward to his attire —dark blue denim paired with a white button-up shirt and a long black coat. Simple but sexy.

He loudly clears his throat, catching me in the act. *Busted.*

His gaze shifts to the ticket clutched in his hand, "Jemma, with a J. This must be yours," he says, almost painfully as he hands some items back to me.

I quickly cram them into my carry-on.

"And you must be"—I glance down at the ticket I picked up—"Luca."

He snatches it from my hand. "I can't miss my flight," he grumbles.

Okay, undeniably sexy, but incredibly rude.

Flustered, I glance around. "This is all the elf man's fault," I insist, pointing down the long hallway.

He follows my gesture, his eyebrows shooting up in curiosity. "Elf man?"

"He was right there," I protest, my cheeks heating with embarrassment. "There was a man dressed like an elf."

He taps his head and smirks. "Maybe we bumped heads harder than you think."

I part my mouth, ready to apologize again, but he turns away, shaking his head as if I'm the craziest person he's ever met.

"Elf man," I mutter under my breath, wondering if I'm losing my mind.

Chapter Six

JEMMA

When I finally reach my gate, the line to board is quite long.

Looks like I didn't need to run like a madwoman after all.

As I weave my way through a minefield of suitcases and people lounging in uncomfortable chairs, I freeze mid-step.

He's. On. My. Flight.

The man I just collided with—Luca—is on my flight.

You've got to be kidding me.

The irony stabs like a pointy candy cane to the cheek. The good-looking, but sourpuss of a man that I just embarrassed myself in front of, is on my long-ass flight to Paris.

Just my merry luck.

In a desperate attempt to put some distance between us, I twist on my heel and pivot over to Jetsetter Goods. After perusing the selection for a bit and splurging on an overpriced bottle of water—because apparently staying hydrated is a luxury—I glance back at the boarding line.

Yikes, it's barely a line at all anymore.

My best friend didn't risk jail time for me to mess up this whole vacation at the last second. I take off in a mad sprint toward the gate.

"Just about missed it," I say, panting, to the attendant.

She nods coldly to the machine next to her, and I proceed to scan my ticket and passport over the little red lights.

The device emits a long, odd beep that makes my heart sink.

You've got to be fucking kidding me.

What's the problem now?

The employee, whose nametag says Judy, snatches the documents from my hand, giving them a once-over with narrowing eyes. She mutters a few words under her breath, then hands the items back to me and gestures for me to continue.

Thank freaking heavens.

Once I finally slip through the boarding door, I let out a breath of relief. *I made it.*

I scurry down the narrow aisle of the cramped airplane, keeping my eyes glued to my boarding pass, trying to avoid awkward eye contact with my fellow travelers already settled into their seats.

When I finally look up, my stomach drops—you've got to be kidding me—it's Luca again. He's lounging smugly in my seat. I glance between my ticket and the seat code above him.

The universe won't give me a break today. I thought it was on my side now.

He's already made himself comfortable in a seat that clearly isn't his, with his earbuds securely tucked in and an e-reader resting in his hands. I clear my throat, hoping to draw his attention quickly, since I'm the last passenger making my way down the aisle. Slowly, he lifts his head, and the moment his frosty-blue eyes lock onto mine, my knees wobble, and I start to second-guess myself. I quickly glance at my ticket again, confirming I'm correct and that I have every right to ask this gorgeous but rude man to move.

"I'm in 24C," I say, with the words coming out more like a question than a statement.

"Oh, Jemma with a J. It's you again," he retorts, flashing his ticket at me. "Looks like I'm in 24C too."

I pull the ticket from his hand. He's right. It says it right there—24C.

I let out a frustrated huff. "There must be some sort of mix-up." Wasting no time, I reach over his head, pressing the call button for the flight attendant.

Seconds later, a petite woman with her hair pinned back in the tightest bun I've ever seen approaches us. "What can I help you with, ma'am?" she asks, eyeing me as if I'm about to cause a scene.

"It seems we're both supposed to be in 24C," I explain.

"I'm sure there's a reasonable explanation for this." Luca flashes her a smile, which shows off his perfectly straight white teeth, exuding a charm that will probably work against me.

She takes our tickets and pulls out her little machine. Her expression tightens, and her nose crinkles. "Uh-oh. It looks like we've made a mistake. We seem to have overbooked this seat. I don't know how that could have happened. I can't believe they didn't catch this at the gate."

"Fantastic," I reply, dying for this interaction to end as everyone seems to be staring now. "I can take any other seat." My shoulders sag.

She taps a few keys on her small machine, frowning as she scans the screen. "It appears we're fully booked. One of you will need to exit the plane and wait on standby."

Luca raises an eyebrow. "You can't be serious."

"I'm afraid I'm quite serious," she counters, her gaze bouncing between us, waiting for one of us to surrender—presumably me.

"Should we flip a coin or something?" Luca suggests with a hint of sarcasm, his accent suddenly thickening.

"No!" I exclaim, tears welling in my eyes. "I used my entire Christmas bonus to buy this flight. I went through hell to get here today. There must be an empty seat somewhere on this plane. I don't understand how this could have happened."

The flight attendant purses her lips. "You can catch another flight. Your ticket won't go to waste, ma'am."

"But I paid a lot of money to be on *this* flight! Maybe he"—I nod to Luca—"can take the next flight."

Luca mutters something that sounds like French and shakes his head.

This isn't how I imagined the start of my trip. I open my mouth, ready to plead my case again when a second attendant comes over and whispers something into Miss Tight Bun's ear.

I catch a fragment of their conversation: "26D is ill. He needs to get off the plane. Now."

Both attendants direct their attention toward a man sitting across the aisle and behind us.

"Let's get you off the plane, shall we?" the second attendant suggests as she skitters behind us.

Our situation gets put on the back burner as they assist the ailing man down the aisle, forcing me to squeeze into a very narrow space, uncomfortably close to the man who refuses to give up his seat. While I can't argue that Luca is undeniably easy on the eyes, my proximity to him makes it hard to think about the irritating situation at hand.

I quickly adjust my gaze to my carry-on, desperate to avoid any accidental eye contact that might add to the awkwardness of the moment.

As the sick man shuffles past me, I can't help but notice —it's the elf man, now dressed in regular, casual clothes. He flashes me a wink as he passes.

Strange.

"It's—" I start, ready to defend my sanity again, but I can already tell I'll sound ridiculous.

Luca rubs a hand over the back of his neck and lowers his gaze. "I'm sorry, but I really do need to be on this flight. I need to get home. I have—"

"Looks like a seat has opened up," the attendant announces, cutting him off and practically startling me to death.

I lose my balance and tumble directly into Luca's lap.

"Oh my gosh. I'm so sorry!" I exclaim, avoiding his gaze

as I leap to my feet. Heat flushes my cheeks, and I'm absolutely mortified for a second time today.

I escape the situation without another word, rushing toward the elf man's now vacant seat.

This is going to be a long flight.

Chapter Seven

JEMMA

Turbulence jolts me awake. I glance up to see the seatbelt sign isn't illuminated, a slight relief given how my body feels—tight and cramped from hours in this seat. I attempt a small stretch, reaching my arms overhead, but the confined airplane seat limits how far I can go.

The pressing need to use the restroom stirs within me, intensifying my discomfort. I shift in my seat, trying to quell the urgency, but it doesn't subside.

I glance over at Luca and see he's fast asleep.

Perfect.

I seize the opportunity to slip past him without enduring another one of our awkward interactions.

I make my way toward the restroom, only to find the line moving at a snail's pace. I shouldn't have drunk my whole bottle of water and the little cup they poured right after take-off. Irritated with myself and everything about this flight, I shift uncomfortably as the line inches forward.

My eyes are fixed on the prize when—tap, tap, tap—I feel a nudge on my shoulder.

I whip around. "Oh, it's you again," I puff, rolling my eyes.

"Moi?" A cheeky grin spreads across Luca's perfectly structured face, and I can't help but notice how infuriatingly hot he looks, even after hours of overnight flying.

"Yes, you seem to be everywhere," I shoot back.

"If I remember correctly, you were the one who ran into me first. And then, you turn up again, requesting *my* seat."

An annoyed huff escapes my lips.

He pushes a wave of dark brown hair off his forehead. "I think we got off on the wrong foot."

"You think?"

"Maybe we should start over. I'm Luca Dubois—and you are?" He gestures theatrically.

What is with this guy? First, I thought he was rude and hated me, and now he's being polite. He's giving me whiplash with his mood roller-coaster. I'm having a hard time reading him, but it looks like I'm stuck here for a bit, and I suppose I started this whole charade by running into him. Plus, he's drop-dead gorgeous. It's not like I can embarrass myself any more than I already have.

"Ugh. Fine. I'm Jemma Jones. That's Jemma with a J," I play along, remembering how he said my name earlier when he passed me my ticket.

"That's a strange way to spell Jemma. Shouldn't it be Gemma with a G?" He raises an eyebrow, still grinning. A single dimple appears when he smiles.

"I thought you were going to be nice now." I purse my lips.

He puts his hands up in surrender. "Sorry, you're right, Jemma with a J. It's a pleasure to meet you." His dark, long eyelashes flutter, making his blue eyes sparkle even under the awful lighting.

I nod, shifting anxiously on my feet as the line inches forward, making me next.

"So, Paris for Christmas?" He tilts his head.

"Yes," I respond.

He rocks on his heels. "Ah, going to have your *Emily in Paris* moment, are we?"

"A *who* in Paris moment?"

"You know—the American show, *Emily in Paris*."

My nose crinkles as the sting of being a workaholic for the past eight years squeezes in my chest. "I have no idea what you're talking about."

"Everybody knows that show," he insists.

"Well, I don't," I snap, my words coming out harsher than I intended.

My annoyance isn't directed at Luca; it's aimed at myself. I've missed out on so much—the dinners with friends and the celebrations I didn't attend. It all stings deeply. I put work before everything else because I wanted to be perfect at my job—diligent, professional, and an over-achiever. I wanted to be the person whom people would admire for her dedication to the company. But at what cost? In the end, it didn't matter. My hard work went unacknowledged, and I ended up getting canned. Plus, my plan backfired on me in other ways I'm not ready to admit yet.

Luca frowns. "Sorry, I didn't mean to offend you. It's just that a lot of Americans seem to really love that show. My city tends to draw a lot of dreamers, you know?"

I nod, keeping my head down, feeling foolish for my overreaction. He has no idea what's going on inside my tightly wound brain.

A wave of relief washes over me when I finally hear the soft click of the bathroom lock. A tall, slender woman wearing a tiny yellow scarf around her neck and a fresh layer of bold red lipstick emerges. She holds the door open for me. I expect Luca to direct his attention toward the beautiful lady, but he keeps his gaze fixed on me, making me a bit flustered.

Luca steps forward with a playful glint in his eye. "Well, if you're not going to—" he says as he grabs the door.

A small giggle escapes my lips. "First, my seat, and now my bathroom? I don't think so." I take the door from his grasp and glide underneath his arm, pulling it away from him.

"Alright, alright. You win," he concedes, stepping back. "Have a fabulous time in Paris, Jemma Jones." He flashes me a wink as I close the door.

What the hell is with this guy?

I hurriedly finish my business and find myself lingering in front of the mirror. I feel self-conscious about the way I look and give myself a pinch in the cheeks to bring some color back. I run my fingers through my hair as I cringe, thinking back to every interaction I've had with the handsome but very frustrating Frenchman. He's cold, then he's hot. But there's something about him that draws me in but also drives me crazy.

Are all French men like this?

Taking a deep breath, I brace myself to see Luca again, but when I step out, he's nowhere to be found. I let out a deep sigh that's surprisingly tinged with disappointment.

Maybe, just maybe, Luca is starting to grow on me.

Chapter Eight

JEMMA

I only have one more encounter with Luca as we shuffle down the aisle to exit the plane. He catches my eye and offers me a friendly smile. And just like that, he's gone, moving ahead with the flow of passengers, blending into the crowd.

Goodbye forever, Luca Dubois.

Once I'm off the plane and through customs, the reality of my situation sets in. I'm in Paris with very little research under my belt, and my funds are limited. As I wait for my luggage at baggage claim, I consider my options: train or taxi.

I should probably save money and take the train, but the lines at the ticket machines are snaking through the terminal, filled with a plethora of tired, confused, and frustrated travelers. Do I really want to be one of those people right now? Plus, I'll have to drag my luggage with me and likely end up nowhere near my rental. I think this is one of those times when it's okay to splurge.

So, taxi it is.

The conveyor belt roars to life, and after a couple of minutes, I spot my luggage making its way toward me. I yank my suitcase from the carousel, follow a sea of travelers outside, and locate the taxi queue.

When it's finally my turn, I greet the driver with a polite "Bonjour," pull out my printed reservation, and show him the address of my vacation rental.

He nods and helps with my luggage as I settle into the backseat.

I'm in Paris. I did it!

A satisfied smirk creeps across my face. I feel like I need to pinch myself to make sure I'm not dreaming. Just a few days ago, I never would have imagined I would be in Paris by the start of the weekend.

I can't wait to get settled in and relax with a book on my balcony overlooking the picturesque cobblestone courtyard. Maybe later tonight I can stop by one of the restaurants on my street for dinner. I'm dying to explore everything around my rental, plus all the major must-sees. I have exactly three weeks to do whatever my little heart pleases—within budget, of course.

I pull my phone from my carry-on, eager to power it on and do a little research, but a memory of Gretchen shifts into my mind: "Don't forget to grab a SIM card when you land."

Crap!

I totally forgot that little detail. If I turn my phone on, I'm bound to get hit with a charge I can't afford. Thank goodness my apartment has Wi-Fi. Once I get settled, I'll look up where to grab a card. Hopefully, there's a store close by.

I slip my phone back into my bag, feeling a little nervous about not being connected. But this is good for me. A true test of my ability to live in the moment.

As we drive, I gaze out the window, mesmerized by the buildings that blur past, and my heart swells with excitement. Everything is so old and, for the most part, well-maintained. The architecture is so stunning it brings me to tears. I've never seen anything like it before. I'm awestruck.

About fifteen minutes into the drive, I attempt to break the silence and make some small talk. However, I quickly realize the driver doesn't speak a lick of English, and I'm too exhausted to practice my French. Maybe after a good night's rest, I'll be more willing to pull some conversational sentences from my brain.

Eventually, we cross over the Seine, and before I know it, the cab driver pulls over, shifting the car into park with a sudden jerk. I scan my surroundings, eager to spot my idyllic vacation rental.

But something seems off.

My eyes dart up and down the street, desperately searching for the quaint apartment building I rented for the month, but it's nowhere in sight.

"Soixante-cinq euros, s'il vous plaît," the driver prompts, extending his hand for his payment.

I again show him the paper with the address, pointing directly to it, hoping he pulled up to the wrong location.

He nods. "Oui."

Unease swirls in my gut as I pass him my credit card. I

crane my neck, still scanning the street for the building pictured in my reservation.

Which one is it?

Noticing the obvious confusion etched on my face, the driver gestures toward the building to the right of the cab as he hands back my card. "C'est ça," he says.

Sure enough, that's the address I gave him.

I swallow hard, my heart sinking to the pit of my stomach.

Hesitant, I get out with my luggage in tow and step onto the sidewalk, staring up at a building that looks nothing like the charming vacation rental I had envisioned. There's certainly no cozy balcony overlooking the street. And where is the cute little café next door?

I take a deep breath and walk up to the building that matches the address printed on the paper in my trembling hand. There must be some sort of mix-up. I'm annoyed, but I suppose I can deal with a misrepresented place as long as there's a bed and a shower with hot water. It's not what I pictured, but it will have to do. I can email them to complain later.

I double-check my instructions. There should be a lockbox to the right of the door.

But there isn't.

The urge to cry swells, clawing at my throat, my breaths coming out in frantic gasps. My skin flushes hot.

I'm so confused.

Desperately, I ring the only doorbell, hoping that maybe, just maybe, I'm overlooking something.

Silence.

I take a step back and study my reservation, comparing it to the building in front of me. They look nothing alike; it's like comparing apples to oranges. Nothing on this stupid piece of paper has anything to do with my booking.

This can't be happening.

I can't even turn on my phone without incurring astronomical charges. I'm furious with myself for forgetting to pick up a SIM card at the airport. And I could kick myself for not doing more research before handing over a large deposit.

Alone in an unfamiliar city and possibly scammed—great.

Chapter Nine

How could I be so foolish?

Nothing good comes from spur-of-the-moment decisions.

I'm a planner for a reason.

I'm a researcher.

I'm a control freak.

This isn't me.

If I had taken the time to plan this trip instead of acting impulsively, I would have done my due diligence and thoroughly researched every little detail. I would have noticed something was off with the listing and moved on to another option. But instead, I stupidly booked what seemed to be the ideal, picturesque accommodation, only to fall victim to a con artist's clever scheme. That's what you get when you decide to fly to Paris on a whim.

What was I thinking?

In a haze, I wander a few blocks before stumbling into

the first hotel on my path. Someone opens the door for me, but I'm too distraught to even look up and thank them. I stroll through an elaborately decorated lobby, clutching my carry-on in one hand and pulling my suitcase in the other. My eyes quickly scan my surroundings, and my chin drops, leaving my mouth agape. If the high ceilings and fancy chandeliers weren't enough of an indicator that this place is out of my price range, the floor-to-ceiling gold mirrors and the grand piano in the corner seal my assumptions.

I gulp, knowing I'll have to fork over some serious cash for a room here. I should just turn around and leave, but it's getting late, and I don't know when I'll come across another hotel.

My skin feels clammy, and I'm desperate for a shower. My shoulders ache from carrying my luggage, and my mind is racing as I try to figure out my next steps, even if that means catching a flight home tomorrow. No matter what, I need to regroup, and this might be the place to do it.

It's only for one night.

I step forward, my black boots clicking against the marble floor as I approach the front desk, meeting the green eyes of the receptionist. "Bonjour," I say, forcing a bright tone.

"Bonjour, madame." The receptionist nods. "Comment puis-je vous aider? Avez-vous une réservation?"

My heart pounds in my chest. *No, I don't have a reservation.*

"Um. Non," I respond, shaking my head.

This would be so much easier in English.

"Um." I bite my bottom lip as my mind scrambles to

form a French sentence, using up my last bit of energy. "Je suis désolée, mais mon français n'est pas très bon. Parlez-vous anglais?" I flash a wide, hopeful smile.

He nods. "Mais bien sûr, madame."

Yes! English!

The words spill from my lips, quick and fiery. "I think I've been scammed. I showed up at a vacation rental down the street, but"—I point in the direction I came from—"it didn't turn out to be what I booked, and I can't even turn my phone on because I forgot to purchase a SIM card." I pass my faux reservation toward him, hoping it will help him understand my situation. "Do you have any rooms available for the night?"

With impeccable posture, he straightens his black tie and locks his gaze onto mine with an intensity that makes me anxious. "Non, ma'am. We're fully booked until the new year, and most of the hotels in the area are at full capacity as well. I know this because I just called around for one of our guests who wanted to extend their stay. You might have some luck outside the city." He takes a deep breath. "Ma'am, I'm afraid to tell you that you're not the first person this kind of scam has happened to. May I suggest calling the number on your reservation to confirm your suspicion?" He places a clunky black office phone on the counter.

I pick it up, dialing the number with quivering fingers. A French version of *this number is no longer in service* plays in my ear.

"The number isn't real," I murmur. "It's a scam." I

shove the reservation back into my bag, but as I pull my hand out, something flutters to the shiny floor.

I bend down, studying the item. It's a piece of paper, a confirmation of sorts, mostly in French. But one thing stands out: the name *Luca Dubois.* And there's a phone number.

"May I use your phone again?" I ask.

He nods, a flicker of sympathy passing through his green eyes.

Against my better judgement, I dial the number, calling the good-looking but irritating Frenchman I met on the plane.

It rings once, then twice, my nerves rattling with each chime.

I should hang up.

What on earth am I doing? I don't know this man.

I pull the phone away from my ear, ready to end the call, but before I can follow through, someone picks up.

"Allô," a thick Parisian voice answers.

"Bonjour. Um . . . is this Luca?" My voice trembles as I clutch the borrowed phone.

"Oui. Who is this?"

"This is Jemma from the airplane. Remember me?" I don't wait for him to answer. "So, I somehow ended up with some of your paperwork when we collided, and it had your phone number on it."

"Oh, I'm sure it's not important. You can toss it."

"Actually, that's not why I'm calling." Before I can stop myself, tears spill over, and I choke on my words.

"Jemma, what's wrong?" There's genuine kindness in his voice.

"I—I think I've been scammed. I'm kind of stranded. I have nowhere to go and forgot to buy a SIM card at the airport. I can't find a hotel room. I'm borrowing a phone. I'm not even sure why I called you." Desperation and embarrassment cling to my voice.

"Whoa. Hold on a second. First, I need you to take a breath."

For some reason, I do as Luca suggests, inhaling deeply, trying to steady my racing nerves.

"I'm sorry you've been scammed. I've heard horror stories of this happening to tourists. And there aren't any rooms around?"

"No, I'm at a hotel right now using their phone, and the receptionist told me all the hotels in the city are booked through the new year. Even if I could find one for the night, I probably couldn't find one for my entire stay," I reply. "I should just get a cab and go back home. I'm so sorry. I have no idea why I called you. I feel silly."

"Eh, don't give up. You're in Paris! It breaks my heart to hear that something so awful happened in my city."

I sniffle.

"Hey, hold tight. My brother, Henri, has a couple of rental properties. I can call him on my other line and see if he has anything," Luca offers.

"Oh. Wow. That would be great. Thank you."

I hear the click as he switches lines.

My heart pounds anxiously in my chest as I wait.

A moment later, his smooth voice fills the phone.

"Jemma, I'm sorry. I knew it was a long shot, but he's fully booked through the new year too."

More tears roll down my cheek. I reach up and wipe them away with the sleeve of my red jacket. "It's okay. Thank you for your help, anyway. I should let you go. I'm sorry to have bothered you."

A hearty chuckle bursts from the other end of the phone. "Oh, I'm not giving up yet. I love a good challenge. Let me come get you. What hotel are you at?"

"You don't have to do that," I protest, biting my bottom lip.

"Just let me at least meet you. I can help you figure things out. I can't let you wander the streets of Paris alone without a plan."

"But you don't even know me," I reply.

"I know we just met, but something tells me you need this trip. Let me help you, Jemma. Plus, I could use the distraction."

I take a deep breath and glance at the receptionist, who's been listening to my entire conversation. "I'm going to pass the phone to the man working at the hotel here, and he can tell you where I am since I have no clue."

After their quick conversation and me thanking the hotel employee a million times, I step outside to wait for Luca. I have no idea how quickly he'll get here, and I don't want to risk missing him. He's my only lifeline in this massive city. I can't believe he agreed to help me, especially after our many awkward interactions. But right now, I'll take any help I can get.

The sun is already setting, painting the sky in warm

oranges and yellows, bathing the street in a soft dusky glow. There's a slight chill in the air, but it's still warmer than New York this time of year, so I don't mind. Since there's nowhere to sit and wait, I pace the narrow sidewalk that's beautifully lined with trees in front of the hotel.

About thirty anxious minutes and a few thousand steps later—though I can't be too sure since I don't have my phone to track anything—a black cab glides to a stop, and Luca steps out.

"Bonjour, Jemma." A soft smile spreads across his stupidly handsome face.

My knees buckle at the sight of him. Just half a day ago, I never thought I would be so excited to see him again—the man I literally ran into at the airport. But here he is, my knight in shining armor—well, more like, savior in a long black coat and a Christmas green scarf with a megawatt smile that seems to light up the whole street.

Swoon.

"Bonjour, Luca." My cheeks flush hot under his gaze. "You have no idea how much I appreciate you coming to my rescue."

"It's no problem at all," he responds, his single dimple taunting me.

I bend down to grab my luggage and try to hide the smile that's claiming my face.

"Let me help you with that," he offers, his English appearing more polished than earlier, as if he's making a conscious effort to mask his naturally thick accent for my benefit.

I take a small step away from my luggage and lift my head . . . right into his chin.

Seriously? How does this keep happening?

"Ouch," I say, rubbing the soft skin around my hairline. Suddenly, a thought strikes me like another blow to the head.

"You lied to me," I blurt out, with zero time to filter my thoughts.

Chapter Ten

JEMMA

"Excusez-moi?" He stares defensively at me while stroking his smooth chin.

"You lied to me on the plane." My voice comes out high and pitchy.

His eyes flicker wildly. "What are you talking about, Jemma?"

My hands drop to my hips. "You told me you had somewhere you had to be, and that's why you couldn't give up your seat. But you're clearly here helping me. So, what's up with that?"

His gaze shifts toward the sidewalk. "It's actually tomorrow morning. I couldn't trust that I'd be on the next flight. It's very important that I am there tomorrow." There's a catch in his voice that makes me believe him. "I didn't mean to come off as a jerk. I've been under a lot of stress."

Guilt bubbles inside of me.

Damn, I'm an asshole.

"I might have come off as a jerk too. I'm sorry. It's been one hell of a week. I shouldn't have called you a liar just now." I nervously gather my long blonde locks, pulling them over to one side.

"So, it's established; we're both a couple of jerks. Now we can move on." He chuckles, letting his baby blues find mine.

I flash him a playful smile, relieved he hasn't decided to up and leave. "Sounds like a plan."

"Shall we?" Luca gestures for me to slide into the backseat of the black cab that's been waiting patiently for us. He grabs my bags, this time without my head getting in the way, and tosses them into the trunk.

I whip around in my seat to watch him, wondering if he's going to join me in the back or post up with the driver in the front. As I wait for him to make a decision, he yanks his phone out of his pocket, with a distressed look falling across his perfectly structured face. He quickly shoves his phone back into his jacket. His sour expression vanishes as he opens the car door. I'm almost giddy when he chooses the back seat. Fresh air invades the car, along with a clean, woodsy scent as he pulls the door closed.

Of course he smells amazing.

"Seat belt." Luca reaches over my body to yank on the belt next to me, allowing his scent to encase me. "It's law here." He grins, locking my belt into place.

"Oh," is all I can manage.

His thigh inches closer to mine, grazing my leg as he leans forward to chat with the driver, leaving me with tingles that sweep through my entire body.

Focus, Jemma.

Luca shifts, turning back toward me, his eyes shimmering. "I'm starving. You must be hungry too."

I hadn't even thought about food, but now that he mentions it, my stomach growls in agreement. I can't remember the last thing I ate, and with the massive time difference, my body feels disoriented. But finding a place to lay my head tonight is my priority, not a meal.

"Shall we grab a bite to eat and then get your situation all sorted?" he asks.

Has he forgotten I'm kind of in the middle of a crisis? Although, I'm not totally ignoring the fact that he wants to eat with me.

"Shouldn't we get me sorted first?" I counter.

He waves me off with a flick of his wrist. "Eh, you Americans are always in a hurry."

I crinkle up my nose. "Well, I feel slightly homeless at the moment. I was hoping to be unpacked and relaxing by now. I'm kind of freaking out. This isn't the start to my trip that I had imagined."

"Hey, no matter what happens, you need to eat, right?"

I really am hungry. I ponder his offer, while I fidget with my hair—my nervous habit.

"I suppose you're right," I finally concede. "But first, can we stop somewhere and get a SIM card? I really, really need my phone. My best friend is going to be freaking out that she hasn't heard from me yet."

Luca looks down at something on the floor of the cab, bends over, and picks up a small yellow bag. He pulls an item out of it and flashes it at me. "I'm one step ahead of you."

Damn, that's thoughtful. Bonus points for Luca.

"Let me pay you back," I say, reaching for my wallet.

"Nonsense. It's my pleasure." He takes my phone from my hands and quickly inserts the card for me.

When he passes it back, I immediately notice a slew of text messages from Gretchen.

> Gretchen: How was the flight?
>
> Gretchen: ????????????
>
> Gretchen: I feel like I should have heard from you by now. Text me.
>
> Gretchen: I tracked your flight. It said you landed. Girl, where are you?
>
> Gretchen: Getting worried. It's been a few hours. Are you held up at customs or something?
>
> Gretchen: Suzy and I are about to go get on a plane.
>
> Gretchen: Just joking. But if I don't hear from you soon, it might come to that. Only half kidding this time.

My poor friend. I didn't think she'd be this worried, but then again, it's the first time I've traveled in a long while, and I'm alone. I quickly shoot off a message to Gretchen before she drags Suzy across the Atlantic in search of her incredibly irresponsible bestie.

Jemma: Sorry!!! I messed up and totally forgot to buy a SIM card and then my rental was a scam. In a cab with a very attractive guy that I ran into at the airport—literally.

Jemma: He's helping me. Long story. Will text you when I know more.

Jemma: Don't worry, I'm safe. I think.

I slip my phone into my coat pocket, feeling a bit better now that I've made contact with Gretchen.

Luca informs the driver of his plans in rapid French, and I struggle to keep up. Unfortunately, my French isn't as good as I thought. Each moment I spend in this city reminds me just how unprepared I am for this trip. What was I thinking?

Go to Paris, Jemma. You'll have a great time. Overpay for a flight at Christmas and get scammed by your impulsiveness. Follow the signs. Yup, Paris is a great idea.

I let out a sigh I didn't realize I was withholding.

Luca reaches over, placing his hand gently on my jacket. "Jemma, this is Paris. Things have a way of working themselves out. Please don't worry yourself."

I take a deep breath, trying to believe him. I sure hope Luca is right. I could really use a bit of Paris magic right about now.

Chapter Eleven

"It's a smidge early for dinner, but I'm still on American time and could use a good meal, so how about we hit up a brasserie?" Luca proposes as we hop out of the cab and onto the sidewalk.

"Early for dinner? It's after five," I shoot back, raising an eyebrow as my stomach growls.

"Ah, that's right; you Americans don't seem to understand the value of a proper mealtime. Now is usually reserved for aperitif—apéro—an appetite kickstarter, if you will. So, dinner doesn't normally start until much later." He wags his finger at me. "But here we say 17:00, not five o'clock. You most certainly won't be eating your dinner at five in the morning." He releases a hearty chuckle.

Ah, Mr. Cocky is back.

"I know that," I snap, letting my hand dramatically fall to my hip. "Cut a girl some slack. It's been a day. That whole I hardly slept since yesterday thing."

"Okay. Okay. I'll cut you some slack." A playful grin dances across his mouth.

"But seriously, I think it's perfectly normal to just eat when you're hungry," I add.

Luca shakes his head. "No matter how many times I've been in the States, I'll never understand your culture." A cockeyed grin takes over his face. "The sheer number of people I saw consuming their meals while at their desks, walking, in cabs, and even on the dirty subway was just mind-boggling. Too much multitasking, if you ask me." He tosses his hands in the air in apparent disapproval. "Meals are meant to be enjoyed, not mindlessly devoured."

"Well, it's a good thing I called you or I would have been walking around the streets of Paris munching on a sandwich like a heathen," I joke.

"I saved you from many a Parisian scowl." He smirks. "But in all seriousness, I don't mean to be disrespectful of your culture, but I fear Americans are missing the whole point of life."

His words are true. Most of my meals in the past year were consumed over my desk. If the crumbs in my keyboard could tell stories . . .

I follow Luca to the rear of the taxi, where he pays the driver. He slings my carry-on bag across his trim body and retrieves my suitcase. His—free hand rises behind me, hovering near the small of my back, guiding me down a picturesque street lined with glowing lampposts.

"So, where exactly are you taking me?" I question as we round a corner, turning into a claustrophobic alleyway. The tall stone buildings swallow the scant moonlight.

"You'll see. It's this way." He gestures.

We walk down an uneven cobblestone path, and after a few steps, I hesitate. I'm enjoying Luca's company, and I appreciate his help, but has my situation clouded my sense of judgment? Should I really follow a man I just met into a darkened street?

My mind races with what-ifs.

He could easily rob me or lead me into who-knows-what.

Trusting tourists go missing all the time, and I'm sure this is how it starts.

But Luca seems too charming to be dangerous . . . right? Although, didn't people say that about Ted Bundy? Ted looked like a killer if you ask me; Luca Dubois, on the other hand, does not. I swallow down the lump that's rising in my throat.

"Jemma, are you coming?" he calls back, breaking through my spiral of self-induced anxiety.

"Yes," I reply, shaking off the horrid thoughts taking over my mind.

Everything will be fine.

"Jemma, I promise you what's through this alley will be worth the short walk." He gestures to the end of the passageway, which I can't see for the life of me. It's too dark.

But I guess I'm already here, so I'm going to trust Luca Dubois, the French hottie. Plus, I don't know if I'd be any better on my own, and Luca has my luggage, so I guess what will happen will happen.

Fingers crossed I don't die tonight.

The absurdity of my situation—my day—and my entire week makes me let out an involuntary sigh. As I do, I trip over a stone hidden in the shadows, lurching forward before regaining my balance just in time.

"Careful, this uneven street can be hard to navigate if you're not used to it." Luca reaches out, extending his hand toward me with a sweet smile.

I accept his offer to help, feeling the warmth of his hand envelop mine. As we finally emerge from the alleyway, I'm pleasantly greeted by a bustling five-point intersection with restaurants at every corner. My shoulders sag with relief as I realize my worries were for nothing. He really is a nice guy, helping me out, taking me to dinner, and showing me his beautiful city.

"Wow, this is incredible," I exclaim, my eyes sweeping over the dazzling garland, spanning from street to street, with twinkling lights elegantly wrapping around balconies and cascading down to the glowing restaurants below.

Despite the chill in the air, countless people are sitting outside, enjoying their beverages and tiny plates of food. It's like something straight out of a holiday painting.

"Jemma, this is Paris," Luca replies with a hint of pride, while making a sweeping motion.

"This is better than I could have ever imagined." I beam.

"I'm glad you're pleased. The trick is to get away from the touristy areas and find the quaint local hangouts. That's how you'll truly experience Paris," he explains, gently taking my arm to guide me into one of the small restaurants with a handwritten chalkboard sign listing the evening's specials.

"You're going to love this place." He grins. "Well, I hope you will. I mean, I suppose I don't know enough about you yet to predict what you'll enjoy. But everyone seems to love it here." He chuckles.

Inside, the host greets us with a nod. He shows us to a cozy little table for two tucked away in the back of the restaurant next to a small, beautifully decorated tree with silver ornaments and white lights.

Luca tucks my luggage into the corner behind our table and pulls out my chair for me.

I'm not sure if it's the romantic atmosphere or the soft glow of the candle on our table or just Luca's kindness, but I think I'm falling for the attractive man sitting across from me. I mean, how could I not?

However, I can't help but wonder if Luca is only being kind out of pity . . . that I'm simply his good deed for Christmas.

I attempt to pull my gaze away before he notices I'm staring, but our eyes briefly meet. The moment sends a surge of desire through me, leaving me blushing like a fool.

To compose myself, I open my menu, forcing my focus onto the foreign words below. As I scan the selections, my mouth waters at the tempting array of options—from crispy duck confit to the classic steak frites—or at least that's all my tired brain can translate right now. I want to pull out my phone and use Google Translate, but I don't want to look silly.

Luca glances at me. "How about mussels to start? The

mussels here are to die for. They make them with white wine, garlic, and herbs."

"Sounds perfect!" I agree, feeling my stomach rumble at the thought. "And then maybe the steak frites for me."

"Excellent choice. I'll have the steak frites, too," he decides. "Shall we split a bottle of red wine too?"

Wine does sound good right about now.

"Sure," I respond, trying not to sound too eager.

With a wave of his hand, Luca calls the waiter back over and confidently places our order. I'm grateful Luca takes charge, sparing me the anxiety of fumbling through my French. I listen closely, memorizing the way he pronounces each word, locking it away for when I dine solo. That is, if I can find a place to stay, or this might be my last and only meal in Paris.

Once the server disappears, Luca leans in attentively. "So, Jemma, are you going to tell me why you decided to come to Paris?"

I open my mouth, but before I can respond, his phone rings. My heart skips a beat as I catch sight of the name flashing on the screen—Colette. A photo of a stunning brunette with sun-kissed skin and a bright smile pops up. He falters for just a moment before declining it.

The waiter promptly returns with our wine, and as he's pouring our glasses, the woman calls again. This time, after declining it, Luca flips his phone over on the table, placing it face down. He reaches for his glass and takes a generous gulp, seemingly ruffled by his relentless caller.

Who's Colette?

I glance at his bare ring finger—no signs of commitment there. Maybe she's just his girlfriend.

I take a deep breath, trying to push aside the sudden pang of insecurity from the attractive caller.

I'm no Colette.

Did I really think Luca was available? A man this handsome and kind-hearted—frustrating but kind-hearted—must have someone special in his life. He looks to be in his early thirties, so he's probably tied down. But then again, I'm pushing thirty myself and still single.

Does it matter, though?

I just met him, and I'll probably never see him again after tonight. But I'd hate for a jealous girlfriend to hunt us down and accuse Luca of cheating or something crazy. Crimes of passion are high in Paris, or so I've heard. I don't want to step on anyone's toes or get between a couple, and I'm most certainly not into a ménage à trois.

Clearing his throat, he nudges the conversation back to me, completely ignoring the fact that he's avoiding someone. "You were about to tell me why you came to Paris."

Nervously, I twist a strand of my hair between my fingers. "I lost my job a couple of days ago," I say in a hushed tone.

"And you decided it was a good time to take a trip?" he quips.

"Kind of." I let out an uncomfortable laugh. "To be honest, I've been a workaholic and never took any vacations. So, when Foster & Sons let me go due to budget cuts, I guess you could say fate led me here. And so far, it's been pretty rocky, as you can see. Some kind of fate, huh?"

His eyebrow quirks up, and he opens his mouth to respond, but the waiter arrives with the mussels. Good timing too; he probably thinks I'm an irresponsible nut. It's better to put an end to this conversation now.

I slide a mussel onto my plate and seize the moment to shift the spotlight. "What were you doing in New York?"

"I was there on business," he replies, leaning back in his chair. "I travel where I'm needed," he says with very little enthusiasm.

"That sounds fun."

"It's not as glamorous as it sounds. Honestly, it's getting quite tiring. I'm thinking about switching things up, maybe finding a new job," he admits, giving me a little shoulder shrug.

"Oh," I respond softly.

I expect him to elaborate, but he doesn't.

Instead, he flashes me a mischievous grin and asks, "What would you want to do if money were no object?"

"Oh, wow. This took an interesting turn." I stroke the stem of my wine glass.

"Well, you just lost your job, so it's time to open up your possibilities, right?" He raises his brow. "So, what is it that calls to you? Like, what's your passion? You can't tell me you were working your dream job." He brings his glass to his lips and watches me while he takes a sip.

I take a generous gulp of my wine, appreciating the full-bodied, earthy flavor, while mulling over his question. I know I wasn't working my dream job, but was my goal of getting into marketing simply settling? I take a deep breath and go for it. I let my wild and crazy dream leave my lips.

"Alright, if money were no worry, I would be a travel blogger," I foolishly admit. "But you've got to travel to blog about it." I let out a nervous, self-deprecating laugh.

"How long are you staying?" he asks.

"I'm leaving on December 26." *Or sooner.*

"Okay, it's settled. Jemma Jones is going to start gathering information for her first blog post: Christmas in Paris."

"I think we're getting a little ahead of ourselves here. First, we should figure out where I'm sleeping tonight."

Luca chuckles. "First, I think you should enjoy your food. What do you think of the mussels?"

I use my tiny fork to scoop out the tender meat and slide it into my mouth, closing my eyes in surprise at the burst of flavor. "Wow. This is amazing."

"I'm pleased you enjoyed it," Luca says with a giddy smile.

"So, have you lived in Paris your whole life?" I ask, keen on switching the focus back onto him.

"Yes, well, most of my life. When I was younger, we lived in Italy for a year. My mother was from a small village in Toscana and wanted to be closer to her family again. But it didn't last long; we all missed France—even my Italian mother." His eyes momentarily flicker. "She was amazing."

"Was?" I ask softly.

"Yes, I lost my mother about five years ago." He doesn't elaborate, and I understand.

"I also lost my mother—three years ago. This time of year hasn't been the same since. I pretty much avoid all things Christmas now."

Wow, I can't believe I just admitted that—out loud— and to a stranger.

"Is that why you're not with your family for the holiday?"

"You could say that. My dad remarried someone much younger, and he's happy, but I'm not. I think he moved on too quickly."

"Oh, I'm so sorry to hear that, but Jemma, life is short. The living should live."

"I suppose you're right." I shift uncomfortably. "I feel bad that I don't visit much. I know my dad misses me, but it's hard to see him settled into his new life without my mom."

"Family can be hard sometimes." He nods, his forehead crinkling as he reaches for the wine bottle.

"You can say that again."

He frowns as silence settles over our table for the first time since we've met. Luca pours more wine into his glass while he studies me. "You're fidgeting."

I crinkle my nose. I hate when people point things out that I'm doing. It makes me insecure, and I hate feeling insecure. I push around the food on my plate before noticing that's a form of fidgeting too. So, I slide another piece of meat into my mouth.

"I'm just getting nervous about finding a place to stay. It's getting late."

I'm halfway through a bite when Luca announces, "You're staying with me tonight."

I choke on my appetizer. "Excuse me. Your translation doesn't seem to be coming across right."

"I have to confess something," he says, his tone turning serious. "I had my brother, Henri, check hotels in the area. The hotel employee you spoke to was right: there's nothing reasonable available tonight. I invited you to dinner to make sure you're not a crazy person before I offered you my place to stay."

"Wait, so you knew when you picked me up?" My mind races to process this information.

"I knew you were having a bad day, and I wanted to help. I knew if I told you right away that your search was useless, you'd have me take you straight to the airport. And you would be missing out on the trip of a lifetime."

"Some trip," I mutter, dropping my head. "I'm in one of the biggest cities in the world, and I don't believe there's nothing available." Agitated, I yank my phone from my bag, desperately scanning for options they might've missed.

I shouldn't have let Luca distract me; I've wasted valuable time.

As the waiter places our main courses on the table, Luca studies me, an amused grin dancing at the corners of his mouth.

"What?" I snap, feeling the heat of his gaze.

"You Americans—always trying to figure out the impossible. C'est comme ça." He chuckles. "It is what it is, and you can't will a different outcome, Jemma."

Ignoring his playful jab, I dive back into my search, fingers flying across the screen.

With each swipe, my heart sinks deeper; utterly unaffordable rooms flash before my eyes. "I think I should leave —go back to New York."

"I think you're making a big mistake," he counters. "What's waiting for you in New York? You lost your job, and clearly, you chose to spend Christmas here instead of with your family. You should stay."

"It's one thing to accompany you to dinner, but it's a whole other thing to sleep at your home, Luca. I can't. That's crazy. We just met."

"I understand, but we're friends now—*amis*. You don't have to decide right now, but I think you'd be making a huge mistake if you went home tonight. Enjoy your meal first, then think about it. I know my word might not mean much, but I promise you I'm not a creep or anything. I'm just a guy extending his kindness to someone who had a terrible week. Plus, it's Christmastime. Everyone deserves a break at Christmas."

"I'll think about it," I respond, draining my glass in one shaky gulp.

Chapter Twelve

JEMMA

Well, it's official: I just might be the dumbest person alive. I'm about to walk into Luca's apartment. The half-bottle of wine I downed at dinner certainly didn't help my decision-making skills. Yet, I'm extremely drawn to Luca, like Santa to a plate of cookies. I want to believe I can trust him. I suppose it's not much different from meeting someone at a bar and then going home with them for a one-night fling. Although I haven't done that since college. Gosh, I haven't done much of anything since college. I deserve to be a bit spontaneous and enjoy this little adventure for what it's worth, right?

I hold my breath as Luca opens the door to his fifth-floor apartment, unsure of what to expect given the fact that we just stepped out of the world's tiniest elevator.

He switches on the lights, and I'm immediately stunned. It's breathtaking. Earthy green colors cling to the walls, while high ceilings stretch overhead, embellished with ornate moldings painted in a soft ivory. It's a bit small by American standards, but large for Paris.

Luca slides off his black loafers, placing them neatly on the mat next to the door. I imitate him, not wanting to be an impolite houseguest. He tosses his keys and wallet into a dish resting on a gorgeous antique-looking piece of furniture and hangs his coat on a wooden coat rack. He thoughtfully moves one of his jackets into a tiny closet to make room for mine on the rack. While I'm fussing with my coat, scarf, and gloves, he takes my luggage somewhere down the hall and returns quickly.

I follow Luca through a beautiful, inviting arched doorway into what appears to be the living room, where a nearly floor-to-ceiling gold mirror commands an entire wall. I quickly scan the room, albeit with a hint of anxiety, desperate not to find anything that could tie back to his mystery caller, Colette. To my relief, the space seems uninhibited by any hint of her presence, easing my mind a little about agreeing to spend the night here.

What's one night? Right?

Luca's home mirrors his impeccable style, with everything meticulously arranged and in its rightful place. A plush white sofa adorned with mossy green throw pillows sits along one wall, while a fancy chandelier dangles from the ceiling over an elegant glass coffee table, pulling everything together at the center of the room. This place totally beats my faux rental.

"No Christmas tree?" I ask playfully, wandering further into the room.

Not that he'd find one in my apartment either.

"Remember, I've been in New York, but I plan to get one soon." Luca strolls over to the marble fireplace, adjacent to the mirrored wall, and lights it.

The logs burst into a crackle and glow red, adding to the dreaminess of his place.

"Your home is absolutely beautiful," I say, my gaze drawn to the two tall windows, free of screens, framing the view outside.

"Ah, the balcony," Luca says, unlatching the windows and pulling them open wide. A crisp breeze waltzes into his home and mingles with the heat from the fire, making me shiver.

He hands me a velvety soft blanket from a woven basket next to the window. I wrap it snugly around my shoulders. Luca takes one for himself and gestures for me to step outside, offering his hand to help me over the narrow window frame. As I step onto the terrace, which has that classic wrought-iron railing that I love, a breathtaking panorama unfolds before me. The Eiffel Tower rises beautifully against the evening sky. The view before me is nothing short of magical.

"It's almost the top of the hour—watch," he whispers, nodding toward the iconic landmark. He keeps his eyes on the black-banded watch around his right wrist.

I wait with bated breath, keeping my eyes pinned on the structure.

"Three, two, one," he counts down, his voice hushed.

On cue, the Eiffel Tower erupts into a glittery display

of lights that glimmer and flicker along the lattice beams and shine like gold against the night sky.

I gasp, completely captivated by the image in front of me. "This is amazing, Luca." A smile creeps across my face, warming me more than the blanket around my shoulders.

Images of the dazzling window display that led me to this very moment swirl through my head, making me question my own reality. Was I really on the streets of Manhattan just days ago dreaming of this exact moment?

I turn to Luca, my heart pounding wildly against my ribcage. We're now face to face, the distance between us shrinking with each fluttering heartbeat. I can almost feel the warmth of his sweet breath mingling with the cold air, creating soft clouds that dissipate between us.

"I'm so glad I stayed."

"I'm glad you stayed too," he responds softly.

For a breathtaking moment, our eyes lock, and I'm engulfed by a rush of emotions. A hopeful, almost reckless, thought flutters to the front of my mind: could he . . . might he kiss me?

The air seems electric, and my entire body tingles with anticipation, as if a thousand sparks have ignited within me, urging me to go with whatever might happen next.

He leans in, and my breath grows ragged with desire.

Is this it?

Is he really going to kiss me?

A jarring sound erupts from his phone, slicing through the charged atmosphere between us.

Frowning, he quickly reaches into his pocket and dismisses a call for the third time tonight.

Has the man ever heard of the silence feature?

All I can think about is the beautiful brunette from earlier, and just like that, our moment is lost—swept away into the dusky night sky.

When Luca looks back up, his expression shifts. A crease deepens on his forehead, and his lips are tight. "It's been a long day. You must be ready to sleep."

Pulling the soft, velvety blanket tighter around me, a small shiver traces its way up my spine. I nod and follow him back inside.

"As I mentioned earlier, I have to be somewhere in the morning, so I'll try not to disturb you. There's a Nespresso machine if you'd like coffee in the morning. Help yourself." He gestures toward the narrow, galley-like kitchen to the left of the living room.

He doesn't elaborate on his plans, and I don't press him further.

"Where can I sleep?" I ask, a small yawn escaping my lips.

"Eh, oui"—he clears his throat—"You can use my guest room. You'll have a private bathroom just to the left of your room. I'll lay out fresh towels for you. My bedroom is the last door on the left if you need anything."

Anything—the offer lingers in the air, but I don't think he meant it the way I'm hoping he did. Why am I falling so hard for a man I just met? Is it the wine—Paris—his kindness?

I muster a platonic smile and follow him down a very narrow hallway.

He pauses in front of my room, opening the door to

reveal a cozy space with a single bed. "It's not much, but it's better than giving up and going home."

While it may not be as nice as the other rooms in the house, he's right; it does beat the alternative. I can regroup and figure out a plan after some much-needed sleep. At least I got to see the Eiffel Tower sparkle.

"It's perfect." I grin.

"I'll leave you to it then. I'm really glad you decided to stay. Bonne nuit, Jemma."

"Bonne nuit, Luca. And thank you again for everything. I really appreciate all you did for me today."

He nods and continues down the hallway. Once I hear his door close, I drop onto the bed.

Am I imagining things?

Did we almost have a moment?

Am I being irresponsible?

Who the heck is Colette, and why does she keep calling?

A whirlwind of thoughts spins through my mind, making me even more exhausted than I already am. I pull out my phone to set my alarm clock for seven a.m. when I'm bombarded with several messages from Gretchen.

Gretchen: OMG are you safe?

Gretchen: You can't tell me you're with a stranger and leave me hanging!

Gretchen: JEMMA!

Oh my goodness. I can almost hear her panicked voice in my head. I should have texted her when I was at the restaurant, but part of me didn't want her to tell me this was a bad idea.

I quickly tap out a response before I give my poor friend a heart attack.

> Jemma: I'm so sorry. The night got away from me.

I pause, fingers hovering over the screen as I think of what to say next. Is she going to think I'm out of my mind for staying here tonight?

> Jemma: So, my day got a bit crazier . . .

> Jemma: Besides getting scammed, which I will deal with later, I couldn't find a hotel. I checked several booking sites, and there was nothing nearby, except for luxury suites costing a few grand a night. If I only knew this city better . . .

> Jemma: I was running out of options and Luca (the guy who's helping me) offered for me to stay at his place. Oh, and he took me to dinner, so I feel like I got to know him a bit . . .

> Jemma: So, it was either go to the airport and give up or stay at Luca's. I chose Luca's. Please don't worry.

> Gretchen: WHAT!!! You're at his house now?

Jemma: Yes! But everything is fine. He's very sweet and kind. His place is so amazing. He has a view of the Eiffel Tower from his living room, Gretch! Plus, he's crazy good-looking. He's French and Italian. The hottest combo there is!

Gretchen: Please tell me you're being smart.

Jemma: I'm in his guest room. I'll lock the door to my room if that makes you feel better, but I don't think I have anything to worry about. Well, except for the fact that he might have a gorgeous girlfriend named Colette who keeps calling.

Gretchen: What! Does she live with him? And yes, please lock your door.

I walk over to the door and flick the lock upward. It makes a slight sound as it latches into place.

Jemma: Door is officially locked.

Jemma: It doesn't look like she lives here.

Jemma: But besides all of that, everything is fine. I'll check in with you tomorrow and let you know my plans. I'm about to fall asleep texting. It's been a really, really, really long day.

Gretchen: Happy to FINALLY hear from you. Glad you're safe. Please keep me posted. I was very worried about you. I expect a morning check-in!!!

Jemma: OK. Goodnight!

I toss my phone onto the bed, my exhaustion fully taking over. I quickly change into my pajamas and crawl under the covers. The mattress is a little firmer than I'm used to, but right now, I don't care. As soon as my eyes fall shut, I'm asleep.

Chapter Thirteen

JEMMA

The next morning, I slowly slide out of bed, wincing as my back protests against the unforgiving mattress. I wonder if a hotel bed would feel the same. Something tells me it would.

I crack the door of the guest bedroom open, straining to listen for any sign of Luca, but the apartment is as quiet as a mouse. He must have left already. He never said when he'd be back, but I imagine I have the apartment to myself for a couple of hours at least. That will give me enough time to figure out my next move.

Now that I'm in Paris, I kind of want to stay, but I can't expect Luca to extend his generosity for the whole month. One night was enough. I should try to be out of here later this afternoon. I don't want to be a burden. Plus, there's the awkwardness of last night that I'm not sure I want to deal with. But if I couldn't find a hotel last night, what makes me think today will be any different?

I slink into the bathroom next to my room, and sure

enough, Luca has set out a fresh set of towels for me, just as he said he would. As I glance in the mirror, my tired, jet-lagged reflection meets my gaze, but something else catches my eye—a note taped to the mirror. I step closer to read it.

> *Good morning, Jemma,*
>
> *I hope you slept well. I'll be back in the early afternoon. Please help yourself to anything in the kitchen. I would love to take you to lunch when I get home. Make sure you enjoy a cup of espresso on the balcony. You'll love the view in the morning!*
>
> *Luca*

I catch a glimpse of the smile spreading across my face.
He wants to take me to lunch.
Maybe there was nothing awkward about last night.
And maybe, just maybe, he doesn't have a gorgeous girlfriend named Colette.
I don't even make it out of the bathroom without pulling up social media and doing a quick search for Luca Dubois. I try three apps but come up empty-handed with each search. Luca seems to be a ghost as far as social media is concerned. I know the French are more private than Americans, but I thought he'd at least have some sort of presence online. This makes me even more curious.
Who are you, Luca Dubois?

I head to the kitchen, overly excited to make myself an espresso and settle on the balcony as Luca suggested in his note. Okay, the fact that he took the time to write me a note when he could have easily sent me a text makes him all the more attractive. The man must have a flaw—I mean, besides being a bit of a know-it-all grump from time to time, but I'll chalk that up to being French. Oh, and the whole he might have a girlfriend thing.

I shrug that little tidbit off my shoulders and pick a pod from Luca's extremely organized coffee station. I'm sliding my chosen espresso pod into the machine when a thunderous pounding erupts from the entryway. I freeze, forgetting to put the cup under the spout. Coffee sputters from the machine, spraying dark liquid across the counter.

Way to go, Jemma.

I grab a towel and toss it on the mess, hoping the person will go away if I don't answer the door.

"Luca!" a woman's voice hollers.

Do I answer it?

My heart races as I tiptoe cautiously through the living room, anxiety coiling tightly in my stomach.

The pounding continues. "Luca, réponds à la porte."

I scramble to translate her words—*Answer the door.*

I really don't want to do that.

After all, Luca isn't here. So, what harm is there in letting it go unanswered? I steal a peek through the peephole, and my heart drops—it's Colette, the beautiful caller from last night. I quickly shrink away from the entryway, wishing I could disappear entirely. I don't want to get Luca in trouble if Colette is his girlfriend. How would she react if another woman opened her boyfriend's door? Did he ever call her back? My guess is no.

"Je pensais que nous pourrions y aller ensemble ce matin," she says, her voice elevated with irritation.

My French isn't as great as I thought, but I think she said something along the lines of: *I thought we could go together this morning.*

What is Luca doing that requires this gorgeous creature to be there too? Whether she's his girlfriend, wife, ex-wife, or the mother of his child—that I've seen no evidence of—my heart sinks.

I don't know what I was hoping for with Luca. I thought maybe the idea of him having a girlfriend was all in my head, but it turns out the sparks I thought we had last night were all in my head.

"Luca!" she calls again, pounding furiously on the door.

Is this woman ever going to give up?

Oh my gosh, what if she has a key?

Would it be worse if she burst in here to find me hiding behind the door?

Ugh! What should I do?

Colette draws my attention back to her with a sharp, "Putain, Luca!

Fuck! I sure hope that means she's ready to give up.

I wait for a hint of silence and then carefully check the peephole.

She's gone.

I rush to the balcony, tossing the window open in haste. I need to get a better look at her.

Ugh! Why am I torturing myself?

I wait patiently, pressing up against the cold window frame, holding my breath, as if that will somehow make me invisible.

After a few moments, an exquisite, tall brunette steps out of the building, wearing a black tailored wool coat over a chunky tan sweater, paired with a knee-length skirt and high boots—the epitome of Parisian chic.

Dang it, she's absolutely beautiful.

Maybe a little hostile, but drop-dead gorgeous, nonetheless.

She pivots in my direction, and my breath hitches, wishing I could slink back inside. She stops, slips on a pair of oversized sunglasses, and glances up in my direction.

Oh crap. Oh crap. Oh crap.

Why did I come out here?

I freeze as our eyes meet—her expression unreadable— maybe surprise, perhaps anger.

Either way, Luca is busted.

Chapter Fourteen

JEMMA

It's all ruined.

Absolutely ruined.

Why did I have to look?

She saw me; she definitely saw me.

I should have stayed hidden behind the door like the good little pity houseguest that I'm supposed to be.

Ugh! Dang it, Jemma!

Do I text Luca and apologize? But for what?

I still don't know who this feisty mystery woman is to him. Maybe I'm overreacting. After all, I've done nothing wrong, except for not answering a door to a home that isn't mine. He'd understand. Right?

Plus, it sounds like Colette is heading to the same place Luca is this morning, so the ball is in her court now. I can't imagine she's going to let this go. It doesn't seem in her nature. I hope I didn't get Luca in trouble after everything he's done for me.

My tortured brain is racing back and forth, but one

thing is certain; my hopes of staying another night seem further away now.

"Why did I have to go and look?" I whisper, slinking back inside, latching the window behind me.

I could really use one of Gretchen's pep talks right about now. I sigh, reaching deep down into the pit of my soul, summoning a dose of much needed positivity. Gretchen would tell me that no matter what happens, I still have this beautiful apartment all to myself for the next few hours and to make the most of it. It would be a shame to not enjoy what's right in front of me.

So, that's exactly what I'm going to do. Well, after I tackle the itty bitty mess I made. Which was not my fault, by the way. It was hers.

After cleaning up the remainder of my spill, I brew a fresh double espresso, this time carefully placing a small white cup beneath the machine's spout. The rich, nutty scent fills the air, making my taste buds itch for the bitter flavor.

With the freshly brewed espresso cradled carefully in one hand, I grab my phone and the cozy, warm blanket from last night, and head back to the balcony. The crisp morning air pecks my skin the moment I cross the threshold onto the terrace.

I've been on this balcony twice now, but it feels like I'm seeing it for the first time. I'm a little less distracted now, so I'm pleasantly surprised to see it's longer than I realized, stretching the entire length of his apartment. At the far end, nestled in the corner against a stone divider wall, sits an inviting metal bistro table with two small chairs.

Squealing with excitement, I drop down onto one of the chairs, the coolness seeping through my thin pajama bottoms. I ignore the slight discomfort because nothing else is going to ruin my perfect Paris morning, as it could be my last. I pull the velvety blanket over my shoulders, letting the excess drape over my legs. Steam rises from my espresso and kisses my lips as I take a sip. Warmth washes over me, spreading through my chest. I lean back, savoring the rich flavor as I turn my attention to the street below. It's startlingly quiet outside for seven in the morning. There's hardly a soul to be seen—so different from the constant hustle of New York City.

I twist in my seat to take a selfie with the Eiffel Tower as my backdrop. I raise my tiny cup of espresso to my lips, ignoring the messy pile of hair atop my head, and snap the photo.

Satisfied, I open my text messages and send the photo to Gretchen.

> Jemma: Is this heaven? No, it's Paris! 🖤

I don't expect her to respond, since it's the middle of the night back in NYC, so I'm surprised when three little dots flicker on my screen. *She's typing.*

> Gretchen: Beautiful! So Jealous! Going back to sleep!

My fingers hover over the screen, itching to keep the thread going, so I can spill my morning gossip, but that will have to wait until it's not an ungodly hour. Instead, I call my credit card company to file a dispute over my rental scam. The woman on the phone is kind and makes it easy to initiate an investigation into the charge. I instantly feel better about the situation, knowing it's getting handled.

My next instinct is to check my work email, but then, like a punch to the stomach, I remember that's not part of my life anymore. The thought almost suffocates me. I'm alone for the first time without the shield of my work. My body begins to tingle with dread.

No job to come back to.

No place to hide anymore.

No more money flowing into my bank account.

I push out a deep, long breath.

I can't go home yet. Things will be so much worse there.

Sighing, I down the last sip of espresso in my cup and open one of the travel apps on my phone.

Minutes tick by as I scroll through listings, coming to the same discouraging conclusion as last night; I can't afford anything that's available. I mean, I could, but only for a night or two. The thought of depleting my savings for a quick fix sends me into a full-blown panic. I know I was ready to hand over all my money yesterday, but now things pinch differently in the light of day. It would be so much easier if I could stay here with Luca.

But as I sit here at this perfectly Parisian table on this ideal Paris balcony, staring at the patchwork of gray, blue, and silver slated roofs with their dormer windows and intricate chimneys forming the flawless foreground for the most iconic structure in the world, I'm reminded I came here for a reason. I haven't found myself yet. If anything, I've become more lost. I need to find the girl I came here for.

One thing I do know for sure: Jemma Jones isn't a quitter. I'm not ready to give up.

Chapter Fifteen

JEMMA

My stomach erupts into butterflies the moment I hear his key sliding into the lock. I rush to the entryway to greet him. I watch as he hangs his coat on the rack, desperate to find out how things went this morning with Colette.

Before I can say a word, Luca's eyes fall to my suitcase sitting next to the door, but he doesn't say anything.

That's not a good sign. He's not begging me to stay.

Okay, okay, I know I said I wasn't ready to go home yet, but I packed so I don't look too presumptuous. After all, he only offered for me to stay one night, and I'm hoping he'll extend his invite for my entire trip. I feel crazy for entertaining the idea. But I really don't want to leave.

I love his apartment.

I enjoy his coffee.

I'm in awe of the views.

And I adore looking at him.

"How did your thing go this morning?" I ask, greeting him with a cautious smile.

He rakes his hands through his dark hair, his face falling slightly. "I'd rather not talk about it."

The stress lines creeping across his face make me think twice about pressing him further. I decide it's best not to bring up his little visitor this morning.

I shift nervously from one foot to the other. "So, your note mentioned lunch," I say, wondering if that's still on the table given his current mood.

"Plans changed," he mutters.

My heart drops to my stomach.

My vacation is over. Hail me a cab, and get me on the next flight home. Au revoir, Paris.

"I'm sorry. I can get out of your hair." I reach for my suitcase.

"I didn't say you need to leave." His brows furrow. "Our plans have changed, as we've"—he swipes in the space between us—"been invited to my brother Henri's home for déjeuner, lunch."

Did I hear him correctly? Lunch with his brother?

I let a soft sigh escape.

The Colette thing must not be a big deal, or he'd let me leave. A sense of hope resurfaces. I bite my lip, attempting to quell the excitement flowing through my body. I want to pounce on the opportunity to ask if I can stay longer, but I want him to come to that conclusion on his own.

"Unless, of course, you have other plans," he adds, knowing darn well I don't have any other plans because if I did, I wouldn't still be here.

"Um"—I rock on my feet, trying to play it cool—"Nope. I'm all yours."

I'm all yours? Did I really just say that?

A sly smile smolders on Luca's lips. "Perfect." He rubs his chin. "I need to make a phone call, and then we'll head out." He walks away, leaving me simmering in embarrassment.

The sound of the balcony latch draws me into the living room, where I catch Luca pacing along the narrow terrace, phone clutched tightly in his hand.

Colette sneaks back in to my thoughts, but I shove her and her oversized sunglasses aside. I quickly busy myself by walking over to the grand antique mirror, where I gather my long hair to one side and weave a loose braid that cascades over my right shoulder, resting along my collarbone. Gazing at myself in the mirror, I notice my lips are pleading for a dash of color. I pull a tube of cherry-red lip stain from my pocket and glide the wand over my lips before pressing them together. With a satisfied nod at my reflection, I stroll back to the entryway, slipping into my long red coat, black scarf, and matching black gloves.

"It's a nice day for a walk if that's okay with you." Luca appears behind me, reaching for his black jacket and this time choosing a gold scarf.

"Oui. J'aimerais ça." I giggle.

"Ah, elle parle une peu français."

"Juste un peu." I squish my gloved thumb and pointer finger together. "I took French in high school and then again in college, but I'm out of practice."

"I'm sure you'll have plenty of opportunity to practice your French while you're here."

Will I?

"Shall we?" I reach for the door.

A silly grin crosses his face.

"What?" I playfully ask, feeling self-conscious.

"You might want to rethink those." He nods toward my shoes.

"What's wrong with these?" I ask, kicking up one of the thin-heeled ankle boots adorning my size seven foot. "I wear these walking all over Manhattan. I'm a pro. Plus, they look cute with my outfit."

"I don't doubt that, but this isn't New York." He grins, studying my face.

"I'm fine," I reply with a rebellious wave of my hand.

"Suit yourself." Luca chuckles, placing his hand on the small of my back, steering me out of the apartment.

About two blocks into our walk, I understand why he questioned my footwear. *Cobblestones! Everywhere!* I thought the little alleyway last night was a one-off situation, but boy, was I wrong.

"You should have warned me," I say, leaning into him for support as my heel wedges between a stone.

"I tried," he quips, steading my wobbling frame with one hand, assisting me down the idyllic, but in my opinion, unfunctional street. A small *I-told-you-so* smile pulls at the corner of his mouth.

"You could have been more convincing," I add, wearing a teasing grin as my heel catches yet another stone. I use the opportunity to cling tighter to him.

I feel his body rumble with laughter. "You're finding this amusing, aren't you?" I tout.

"Is it that obvious?" He grins, his single dimple mocking me.

"Okay, so maybe you were right." Leaning into him, I take a deep breath, expecting a whiff of Luca's intoxicating scent, but instead I'm greeted with a burst of buttery goodness mixed with toasted bread and spices—a pleasure for my senses.

I look up to find the quaintest little boulangerie with patrons spilling out of the building. Full tables of content people, laughing and chatting without a care in the world, line the narrow cobblestone passageway.

"Hello, Paris! Nice to meet you." I make a sweeping motion with my free hand.

Luca bursts into a boisterous laugh.

"What?" I question.

"I like experiencing Paris through your eyes."

My cheeks redden as I attempt to control the smile overtaking my face, but I can't hold it back any longer. "This place is something else, Luca. I can't believe you get to live here and experience all this beauty every day."

"C'est Paris," Luca states proudly.

I'm in absolute awe of everything we pass, from the magnificent stone buildings to the fabulous boutiques and restaurants, all beautifully decorated for Christmas. I mentally note them all, creating an itinerary—if I stay. And right now, that's a big *if*. But he clearly doesn't seem like he's in a hurry to get rid of me.

"So, how far away is your brother's place, anyway?" I pull back to look him in the eye.

"Not far for someone in flats." He smirks.

I playfully nudge my shoulder into his. I know we've just met, but I feel like we've quickly fallen into a rhythm.

Luca clears his throat. "We're in the sixth arrondissement—think of it like a neighborhood."

I tilt my head toward him, twisting my mouth upward. "I know what an arrondissement is, thank you very much."

"Okay, okay. Not everyone's an expert like you." He laughs, tossing his free arm into the air. "So, we're in the sixth, and Henri lives in the fifth, the Latin Quarter. We're left bank kind of guys. Always have been, always will be." He chuckles.

"I can see why," I add, my gaze floating from one dreamy building to another.

"I thought since it's a nice day, we could cut through the Jardin du Luxembourg. Snap a few photos for your blog"—he winks at me—"then it's just a few more blocks."

"I still don't know about the whole blog thing, but I'd love to see the gardens."

"Eh, come on, Jemma. You said you want to write a travel blog. You're traveling, so blog about it. Easy."

"It seems like a waste of time, since I won't be able to keep up on it when I get a new job." My stomach dips at the thought of starting from the ground up all over again.

Tension seeps back into my bones. The carefree Jemma from moments ago is quickly replaced with the overthinker shell of a person I've been for the past few years. My face drops, and my pace stalls.

"I'm sorry if I've said something to upset you," he says, matching my pace.

"It's just that I forgot I'll be starting over with vacation time, along with everything else. I'll be lucky if I get two measly weeks. Some companies make you jump through hoops just to earn that." I let out a dramatic sigh.

Luca shakes his head. "That's so depressing. We get five weeks off, plus eleven paid holidays. I'm actually on holiday right now. As a matter of fact, I'm taking the rest of the month off."

"The rest of the month?" I gasp.

"I earned it." He flashes me a quirky grin. "I wanted to take the rest of the month off, so I am."

I scrunch my face upward. "Okay, you can quit rubbing dirt into my wound any time now."

"In France, we work to live, not live to work. Joie de vivre; it's the French way."

"Well, I might have to move to France then."

"Maybe you should." He playfully bumps his shoulder into mine.

My pulse races at the thought. "If only it were that easy."

"If you want something, Jemma, you have to make it happen. Like your blog. Just make it happen."

"Now you sound like my best friend, Gretchen."

"Gretchen sounds like a smart girl."

"Gretchen's great. She's the reason I'm here right now. Well, she's the one who put the seed of the idea in my head."

The reason the seed grew is a much longer story and a

little unbelievable. Fate, magic, Santa—eh, either way I'm here.

Luca turns to me, his blue eyes shimmering. "I'm glad she did," he responds, and my insides turn into mush. "And if you wouldn't have lost your job, by the sounds of it, you wouldn't be here either. So, it's a good thing you got fired, right?"

"I'd prefer not to be homeless in a few months, so I don't know if I'd go that far."

"Everything happens for a reason, mon petit lapin."

Did he just call me a little rabbit?

The brisk air kisses my cheeks as we enter the Luxembourg Gardens, arms still linked. I don't feel the need to pull away, and it seems he doesn't either. I like being close to him. He makes me feel safe.

Luca offers several facts about the gardens as we pass by happy people munching on baguettes and sipping wine from real glasses—not those flimsy plastic cups. People-watchers are perched on green metal chairs and benches, while tourists wander the park with their phones glued to their hands, taking pictures of everything in sight.

Which reminds me.

I slyly slip my fingers into my clutch and fish out my phone. As we walk, I snap a few photos of the scenery and some statues, but what my fingers are really itching to capture is a shot with Luca. If today is the last day we see each other, I want proof he existed. I want a memory of him, but how do I do it without looking like a total creeper?

As if reading my thoughts, Luca reaches for my phone. "Shall we?" He turns us around, and before I can even nod, he leans in and snaps a selfie with the Luxembourg Palace behind us, forming the ideal backdrop.

When he hands my phone back, I gleam with giddiness at the image staring back at me.

Gretchen's getting this photo pronto!

> Jemma: We make a cute couple—even if Luca doesn't know it yet.

I click *send*, and immediately my phone buzzes with a response.

> Gretchen: Hello, handsome!

I catch a smile forming as I slip my phone back inside my purse. The park finally spits us out to a busy street, where I spy several hotels in the distance.

"Think I should pop in and see if there are any vacancies?" I ask, with zero desire to follow through.

"We'll deal with that later—we're going to be late."

"Luca, I'm falling in love with Paris more and more with every step. I'm not ready to go home." I gesture to the street around us.

"Jemma, I told you things have a way of working themselves out in Paris. Everything will be fine."

But as the words leave his mouth, his phone rings.

Chapter Sixteen

JEMMA

How is everything going to be fine when *she* keeps calling?

Once again, he declines the call, the screen darkening as he slips the device into the pocket of his black jacket. His stance turns rigid as I let my arm fall from his, the cool winter air seeming heavier now.

Part of me wants to scream, "Who is Colette?" But another part of me doesn't want to rock my unstable boat. I have a good thing going here with Luca, and I don't want to ruin it by being nosy. It's none of my business how he conducts himself with the people around him. Plus, I just met him, so he owes me no explanation. He's a big boy. He can make his own decisions, but I feel like I'm doing something wrong by staying in his home, having lunch with his family, and . . . falling for him.

Am I being totally crazy?

I leave right after Christmas—or sooner—so is it even worth asking the questions that are searing a hole in my mind? I need to accept what this is: a man being kind to a down-and-out tourist during Christmas.

But I did feel sparks between us. I'm not imagining that. I'm not crazy. And I can't ignore the fact that I'm falling for him—hard.

How can I have such strong feelings for someone I just met? I've never felt like this in my entire life. There's something about this man that I crave like an addiction. I know I could easily walk away and into one of the many hotels behind us and hope something opens up, or I could book a flight back home, but I physically can't. My feet won't allow it. I need to see whatever this is through to the very end.

My eyes slowly wander to Luca, and for the first time, I see something that I haven't before—a sadness—a pain behind his frosty blue eyes. Something in my heart tells me Colette is to blame.

I part my mouth, unsure of the words that need to come out, but Luca beats me to it.

"We're here," he announces softly, stopping in front of a building with a creamy stone façade and vibrant blue double doors.

He pauses, staring straight ahead, his eyes pinned on a massive, ornate metal knocker adorning one of the doors. "Sorry if I've seemed a bit distracted at times. I have a lot on my mind these days."

"The reason you had to be on that flight?" I softly question, my gaze dropping to my feet.

He nods. "Jemma," his voice hitches.

This is it. He's going to tell me he made a mistake and that I should go.

My heart crumbles.

He clears his throat. "I know we just met, but I was wondering"—he rubs the back of his neck, moving his gaze to mine—"if you'd like to be my guest until you leave at the end of the month. I have plenty of space and a spare key, so you could come and go as you please."

My mouth drops.

It's everything I've been wanting, but one question lingers: am I only a distraction?

"Yes," the word tumbles out of my mouth. "I'd love to stay. I could pay you. Although, it wouldn't be much."

"Nonsense. It would be my pleasure to host you."

A crack of a smile simmers at the corner of my mouth. "You have no idea how much I appreciate this. Are you sure I won't be in your way?"

"Absolutely not. To be honest, I could use the company. It will be a nice distraction having a roommate around."

Distraction. Roommate.

There it is. I'm a distraction from whatever is going on in his life. But I can't look a gift horse in the mouth. I need this. So, I guess we're both kind of using each other then. I don't know what kind of mess I'm getting myself into, but I'm willing to go with the flow if that means I can stay.

Chapter Seventeen

JEMMA

"So, are we just going to stand outside all day?" I laugh, rocking back on my heels.

I expect Luca to use the eye-catching door knocker, but he opts for the keypad to the right of us. As he taps a couple of buttons on the pad, I step back and gaze up at the Juliet balconies jutting out from the upper floors.

"It's so charming," I whisper into my scarf as a breeze drifts past me.

The lock emits a soft click, and Luca yanks the large door open. I follow him into a courtyard where the winter sun fights through the tall buildings, begging to shine across the cobblestone path—*yes, more cobblestone*s.

Multiple pathways crisscross through the small space, leading to different doors, but we take the path straight ahead.

With a quick knock, Luca steps back, and the door swings open to reveal a tall, fit man with dark hair like

Luca's, except with a soft sprinkling of gray. "Coucou, mon frère!" the man exclaims, yanking Luca into a tight hug.

"Salut, Henri!" Luca replies cheerfully, leaning in.

When they finally pull back, Henri smiles strangely at me, eyeing me up and down.

"Bonjour," I shyly offer, tugging on the loose ends of my braid.

"Eh, oui. C'est mon amie, Jemma," Luca introduces me in French.

Does his brother not speak English? This should be interesting.

"Elle est jolie," Henri says with a cheeky grin, elbowing Luca playfully.

My cheeks heat up—did he just call me pretty?

I sneak a glance at Luca, who's grinning wildly.

"Oui," Luca admits. "Je suis d'accord."

I hold back the smile that's threatening to take over my entire face.

Luca thinks I'm pretty! Luca thinks I'm pretty!

Henri waves us inside, and as we slide past him, I tilt my head back, leaning into Luca to whisper, "Tu sais, que je parle un peu français, non?" *You know I speak a bit of French, right?*

Cocking his head to the side, he replies, "I know." His lip curls into a sultry grin, letting his eyes linger on mine longer than necessary, stirring a craving in me that makes me burst from the inside out.

Is it bad that I want to rip his clothes off right here and now?

Calm down, Jemma.

At first glance, Henri's place is smaller and much darker than Luca's flat. I suppose it's the ground floor letting in less light. It's nice, but I prefer Luca's place.

"So, you're the one that got scammed, huh?" Henri asks, coming out of left field, speaking perfect English, pulling me back to the reality that set this whole thing into motion.

I feign a pout. "Yes. But thanks to my knight in shining armor, I didn't have to sleep on the street!" I giggle, playfully leaning into Luca, letting my arm fall to his bicep.

A funny grin crosses Henri's face, but before I can ask him what's up, two young bundles of energy burst out from one of the backrooms.

"Jemma, these are my sons, Elias and Mylan," Henri offers.

"Hello," they chirp in unison.

"Mylan's my oldest; he's nine. Elias is seven," Henri adds, ruffling the taller one's hair.

"Are you from America?" Elias asks with a soft accent.

"Yes, I'm from New York," I reply, kneeling slightly to meet his blue-eyed gaze.

"Wow!" Elias gasps. "I've never met anyone from New York before."

"Well, I'm pleased to be the first New Yorker you've met. And I must say, you speak English really well."

Elias smiles, revealing a missing front tooth. "Really? You think so?"

I nod enthusiastically. "Absolutely."

"We're learning in school," he states proudly, puffing out his little chest.

"Red or white?" Henri interrupts, flashing me two half-filled glasses.

"She'll take the red." Luca reaches for the glass, swirling the liquid before passing it to me.

Oh dang. He knows me so well already. Total turn-on.

"Merci," I respond, tilting it toward my host.

"Can I see Jemma my room?" Elias winces, presumably noticing he messed up his English.

"Sure. You can *show* Jemma your room," Henri responds, correcting Elias.

Eagerly, the boys lead me down a narrow, dark hallway and into a small room with two neatly made beds. It's simple yet tidy; everything has a home, perfectly in its place, just like their Uncle Luca's home.

Taking a large gulp of my wine, an untamed thought flits through my head. "Hey, can I ask you boys a question?" I glance between the two of them.

Mylan and Elias excitedly nod.

I step further into the room, careful that my question won't be overheard. "Who is Colette?"

"Eh . . . um," Elias stutters, letting his gaze drop. "Dad said we're not supposed to talk about her around Luca."

"Oh? Why is that?" I press gently, feeling ridiculous for trying to press an answer out of these sweet innocent boys.

"Because Colette and Luca are"—he looks to his brother—"what's the word, Mylan?"

"Fighting," Mylan responds, playfully punching the air. He giggles, tossing himself onto one of the neatly made beds.

"Fighting," Elias repeats under his breath, as if he's

locking the English word into his memory. He's a smart kid.

It's several seconds before my mind wraps around the word. Fighting. A partial fit of relief withers through my veins, making me feel less guilty for the desires coursing through my body.

"Why are they fighting?" I probe deeper, desperate for more information.

"I don't want to talk about that. Can I show you my toys instead?" Elias takes my hand and leads me to a wooden toy chest.

"Of course." I smile.

He drops down to the rug, swiftly plunging his hands into the deep box.

As I wait for him to resurface with something grand to show me, an object catches my eye. Above the chest, resting on a beautiful wooden shelf, is a framed photograph. Reaching up, I pluck the frame from its place. A woman with mid-length dirty-blonde hair, vibrant red lips, and wide blue eyes caught mid-laugh stares back at me.

"Is this your mom?" I ask, flashing the photo at the boys, realizing I haven't seen anyone else in the apartment. It didn't even cross my mind to inquire further about Luca's family.

"Oui, c'est ma maman," Elias responds, switching to French without noticing.

"She's very pretty," I respond, setting the photo back in its place.

Elias giggles.

"Where is she?" I ask.

"Um." He bites his bottom lip. "I don't know the word. Sorry, I keep forgetting." He looks to his brother once again for help, but Mylan shrugs his shoulders.

"Eh." He bites his lip. "She's with grand-mère." He points upward.

My hand flies to my mouth.

Luca's mom. Heaven.

These poor sweet boys—their mother is in heaven with Luca's mother, their grandma.

I swear I feel my heart split in two.

Geez, what's wrong with me? Could I traumatize these boys anymore? Have I lost all my tact?

Quickly, I replace the photo on the shelf, just in time too. When I look over my shoulder, Henri is leaning against the doorframe, eyeing me strangely again.

Did he hear me interrogating his children? Just let the ground open and swallow me whole. I'm making a great first impression on the Dubois family.

"Let's let Jemma get back to the adults now, shall we, boys?" Henri says.

Elias mutters something in French and frowns.

"I hope they weren't too much of a handful. I would have rescued you sooner, but I had to get the table set."

They were the ones who needed rescuing from me.

"No, not at all. They're very smart and sweet boys."

With a heavy exhale, I join Luca, who's already seated at the table that looks like it's set for royalty, not a small family lunch.

Several serving trays line the middle of the table, mostly seafood, including escargot, which makes my stomach churn at the sight of them. Where did all this food come from? I swear it appeared out of thin air.

"Wow, this is all for lunch?" I whisper, dropping into my seat.

"Oh, no. This is just the first course." Luca laughs.

"Oh." I bob my head.

Mylan and Elias are fighting over who gets to sit next to me when the front door creaks open, admitting a blast of cool air into the house. I lift my head, and my mouth falls open.

An eerily familiar looking blonde haired woman glides into the room, positioning herself at the end of the table.

I stiffen in my seat, and my breath hitches in my throat.

"What's wrong? You look like you've seen a ghost," Luca asks.

I open my mouth, but the words don't come out.

"Do you know Mia?" Luca questions.

"I thought she was dead," I whisper as low as I possibly can, so no one else can hear.

Chapter Eighteen

JEMMA

Luca blinks at me, completely baffled. "Why on earth would you think that?"

I swallow hard. "Elias said his mother was with his grandma, and then he pointed up." I mimic the kid, using my pointer finger. "Heaven." I gulp. "With your mom."

Luca lets out a lively chuckle, everyone turning their gaze to us.

He leans in and whispers in my ear, his breath smelling of rich wine. "His grandmother, Mia's mother, lives upstairs. Both very much alive, I assure you."

"I see that. Now."

The boys stop fidgeting next to me and dash over to their mother, excitedly shouting, "Maman."

Relief and joy flood me.

"Jemma, voici ma belle-mère et ma femme, Mia," Henri says, introducing me to his very much alive wife and mother-in-law. "They don't speak much English," he adds.

His wife is beautiful in that *I woke up looking like this*

kind of way with her full shoulder-length blonde hair artfully disheveled, yet perfectly styled, natural-looking makeup, except a dash of red across her thin lips, wearing casual jeans, white sneakers, and a blazer thrown over a white, boxy tee. Simple, but utterly stunning. The grandmother is just an older version of Mia, but slightly more elegant and donning a little more makeup, with the evidence caked into her laugh lines.

"C'est un plaisir de vous rencontrer," I stumble over my words, but I'm pretty sure I said it was nice to meet them.

Our meal plays out for another two hours and mostly in French. Luca is kind enough to pause every so often to translate snippets for me. I don't bother to pay attention or keep up with the conversation; their rapid-fire French is a little too much for me. But the red wine and the bœuf bourguignon are more than enough to keep me entertained. The dishes seem to multiply, a continuous parade of new-to-me cuisine. Just when I think there can't be anymore coming, a cheese plate is set in front of me.

I might burst if I eat another bite, but I don't want to seem rude, so I take a little nibble.

Seriously, how do they all stay so fit when they eat like this?

"I hope you saved room for dessert." Henri comes up from behind me, setting some sort of puff pastry in front of me.

Okay, it's official—I'm going to burst. There's no more room for this food. I smile and graciously accept the elegant pastry with zero intention of consuming it.

As I absentmindedly poke at the puff with my fork,

Elias—who managed to win the spot beside me—asks a question, taking me completely off guard. "Do you love Christmas, Jemma?"

"Eh . . . um"—my gaze drops back to my plate"—I used to really love Christmas." Under the table, I wring my hands together nervously.

"Used to?" he presses, his voice soft and sweet.

Ugh! Why did I say that?

I want to reel the words back in. I've had too much wine.

Elias blinks, waiting for my response.

I swallow down the lump lodged in my throat. "Um—well, Christmas was my mother's favorite holiday. Since she passed away, I can't bring myself to enjoy it anymore."

"Je suis désolé," Elias whispers. *I'm sorry.*

"What was her favorite part of Christmas?" Mylan chimes in, clearly too naive to read the room or notice the massive frown clinging to my face.

"Christmas cookies." The words catch in my throat as tears threaten my eyes.

I quickly divert my gaze to my nearly empty wine glass, desperate to keep my tears from spilling over. If I make eye contact with anyone around the table, I won't be able to hold it together.

"Cookies?" both boys question, their voices coming together in a curious harmony.

"Yes, cookies. My mom and I would spend an entire day making Christmas sugar cookies using insanely old cookie cutters and a recipe that was passed down from her mom, my grandma. We would make dozens of snowmen, trees, snowflakes, and reindeer, and then we'd decorate them with an icing recipe that was mostly powdered sugar, but it tasted delicious. To be honest, the whole recipe was mostly sugar and Crisco, but it was so good." I nervously stroke the stem of my wine glass. "We would dance and sing along to Christmas music while my dad taste-tested. He called it quality control. My mom would slap his hand when he got too greedy. Those were some of the happiest times of my life." I can't believe how this memory pours out of me, as if it's been locked away deep inside, just waiting to spill out.

When I look up, Luca's watching me.

Reaching for my wine, I lift the glass to my lips and take a small sip, as it's all that's left.

Luca reaches under the table and grabs my hand, squeezing it tight. His touch makes me want to melt into my chair.

"Henri, remember how much Mamam loved the Christmas markets?" Luca asks.

Henri smiles, nodding.

"She used to drag us to every market in Paris. She loved the one at the Tuileries Garden. We always had to get there while it was still light out, so she could map out her plan, and then we'd stay until the very end. I remember one year when we had to literally pull her to the exit."

"That was her last Christmas," Henri adds.

"It's like she knew." Luca takes a swig of his red wine.

This time, I'm the one squeezing Luca's hand.

After lunch, I'm left alone at the table with Mia and her mother, while the Dubois men insist on clearing the table. I refill my glass, nodding and smiling along to a conversation that I struggle to follow. I catch bits and pieces. I'm pretty sure they're saying how much they pity me. But either way, they seem to have their own language, and I don't just mean French.

Determined to make myself useful, I grab one of the serving dishes and head toward the kitchen. As I round the corner, I notice both Luca and Henri leaning against the counter, facing the window that overlooks the courtyard, engaged in what appears to be an intense conversation. Not wanting to interrupt their discussion, I quickly set the dish down, still going unnoticed.

As I pivot to leave the room, out of the corner of my eye, I watch Henri lean into his brother. In a hushed voice, he whispers something. The only part I can translate is, "You need to tell Jemma."

My chest tightens. *Tell me what?*

Chapter Nineteen

JEMMA

The walk home is quiet.

Luca hasn't said much since we left his brother's house. I keep stealing glances at him, trying to figure out what's changed. His mind seems far away, and his expression is just as distant.

Does this have to do with what his brother said in the kitchen—"You need to tell Jemma"? Part of me would rather not know what Henri meant, since I have a place to stay now. But the part of me that's falling for him needs to know. Could it have something to do with Colette?

As the last bit of daylight falls behind the horizon, because apparently lunch is an all-afternoon event in France, I bite my bottom lip, mustering up the nerve to ask him, hoping I don't regret it.

Clearing my throat, my question tumbles out, "What were you and your brother talking about in the kitchen? It seemed like you were deep in conversation."

His eyes remain fixed ahead. "You were in the kitchen?" he asks, his tone evasive.

Answering a question with a question—not a good start.

"I wanted to make myself useful, so I brought in some dishes."

"Oh." He nods thoughtfully, but still offers no answer.

"I heard my name before I left," I press.

Straight-faced, he responds, "Everyone was talking about you all day. It's uncommon for one of us to bring someone new around. I'm sure Henri was just saying how well the boys took to you. That's all."

Suddenly, I'm questioning whether I heard the words that I thought I heard. I've been paranoid since I arrived. Maybe I'm self-sabotaging a good thing. After all, I'm not fluent in French. I probably misheard or misinterpreted the conversation. I should feel flattered that he brought me home and everyone—well, the English speakers—seemed to enjoy my company. And the boys did say Colette and Luca are fighting, so perhaps there's nothing left to discuss, anyway.

A flicker of contentment washes over me, reminding me that all this anxiety might be a product of my own wild imagination.

I open my mouth, ready to change the subject, but Luca cuts me off.

"I have some things I need to take care of." He abruptly stops on the sidewalk, catching me off guard.

I'm sure the look of disappointment etched on my face is strikingly clear under the pale glow from the picturesque lamppost he chose to stop beneath.

"Do you remember the way to my apartment from here?" he asks casually.

My stomach contracts. Why does he want to leave me? Is it because of what I just asked him?

I nod, pulling my coat tighter around me as gray, angry clouds and wind roll in, as if mirroring my feelings.

He reaches his hand into his pocket and passes me a key. "The code for the main entrance is 0830, and this key will get you into my apartment. I'm not sure how long I'll be, so don't wait up. Just leave the apartment door unlocked for me, alright?"

I nod once more, stunned in place.

"I'll get you your own key tomorrow. That way, you can come and go as you please. And if you need to leave for dinner—"

"Oh, there's no way I can eat another bite tonight," I interrupt, managing a small laugh to mask my discomfort. "I think I'll probably spend the evening job hunting and then turn in early. The jetlag is catching up with me."

Lies. All Lies.

Luca frowns slightly. "But you're on vacation, Jemma. I wish you'd enjoy yourself more while you're here."

I huff. "I'd enjoy myself more if you weren't abandoning me on the street corner."

"It-it's not like that," Luca stammers.

I pivot, twisting on my heels, unable to hold back my emotions any longer. "It's fine. You don't owe me anything," I say under my breath as I dash away into the darkness, tears pooling in my eyes.

Chapter Twenty

JEMMA

A clanking sound jolts me awake. Startled, my mind falters for a moment, forgetting where I am. The pieces slowly form in my sleep-addled brain.

Paris. Luca's apartment.

A flash of a memory from last night walking away from Luca clocks me. When did he come home?

I stumble out of bed, my eyes adjusting to the golden light streaming through the window. I crack the guest room door open; the intrusive sounds continue.

What on earth is going on out there?

"Luca! It's like seven a.m.! What's with all the racket?" I grumble, still unsure of what to make of him leaving me last night.

No response.

As I navigate my way down the narrow hallway, the chevron floorboards creak beneath my cold, bare feet.

"Luca?" I continue through the living room area.

Still no response, but I hear another clatter, more like a clank of something hitting the ground. I turn the corner into the galley kitchen, where I find Luca bent over, his back to me, fingers hastily gathering something from the floor. He doesn't know I'm here.

I clear my throat.

He quickly stands and whips around to face me with a baking sheet in his grip. His eyebrows practically leap off his forehead when he catches me staring at him.

"Um . . . Jemma," he stammers. "I—I didn't think you'd be awake yet."

"Well, it's kind of hard to sleep with all the ruckus you're causing," I retort, my eyes drifting down his body. My mouth falls open in shock when I see what he's wearing.

"You like?" he asks, a sly grin plastering his face.

I erupt into laughter. "What are you wearing?"

His face flushes bright red, matching the Santa Claus apron tied tightly around his incredibly toned physique, hugging him in all the right places.

"I got you one too." He sets the baking sheet down and presents me with a similar apron, this one emblazoned with Mrs. Claus.

"What's this for?" I ask, trying to stifle my giggles.

"I scoured the internet, searching for American Christmas sugar cookie recipes and even managed to track down most of the ingredients." A proud look crosses his handsome features. "I hope it's close to the one your mom used to make—the one you were telling my nephews about." He steps aside to reveal the small countertop behind him, overstocked with cookie cutters in festive shapes, ingredients, and all the necessary supplies.

Everything looks brand new.

Did he go out and buy all of this just for me? Is this what he dashed off to do last night? If so, his communication could use a teensy tiny upgrade, but I can't be angry. I don't have words—I'm shocked.

Tears spring from my eyes.

Without one iota of thought, I spring toward him, tossing my arms around his neck. "Oh, Luca. This is the sweetest thing anyone's ever done for me."

His clean, woodsy scent wraps around me like a gift, making it nearly impossible to release him. I let the hug linger a few more moments before pulling back to meet his gaze.

"I was worried that I might have gotten carried away, and you would think I'm overstepping." His eyes glow with relief. "After hearing you talk to my nephews yesterday, I thought it might be time for you to bake again." He swallows hard, his Adam's apple bobbing in his throat. "I want you to experience the joy it once brought you—in honor of your mother, of course. I'm sure she would want you to carry on her tradition. I know my mother would want the same."

"Thank you," is all I can muster as tears spill down my cheeks, carrying away all the doubt I had last night.

"You're sure you're not upset?" he asks gently.

Reaching up, I pat the palms of my hands against my

cheeks, trying to wipe away the tears that have taken over. "No, not at all. The truth is, I didn't realize how much I had been missing these little things until yesterday. Avoiding them seemed easier, you know?"

Luca nods sympathetically.

"I always thought moving on would mean forgetting her. But now, I'm starting to realize that by not moving forward, I might actually be forgetting her. Does that make sense?"

"It makes total sense, Jemma. Everyone copes with death in their own way."

"I'm not sure if what I did could really be considered coping," I respond with a sigh. "I threw myself into my job, allowing no free time to grieve. I even stopped celebrating Christmas. It didn't seem fair that my mother could no longer enjoy her favorite holiday, while I carried on without her." I slowly shake my head.

His eyes search mine. "May I ask what happened?"

"Accident." My words come out hushed—foreign— like they don't belong to me. "My mom didn't even have a chance to react. It was raining so hard, and the other driver . . ." I can't finish, the words choking in my throat.

Luca wraps his arms around me, pulling me close to his chest, his heart pounding in rhythm with mine, as if our hearts are beating as one.

"That's awful," he murmurs softly, his breath warm against my messy morning hair.

I pull back just enough to meet his frosty blue eyes. "She would have loved you."

A tender smile crosses his full lips.

"How did I get so lucky running into you?" I ask.

"It was all the elf man's fault, remember?" He chuckles. "Why don't you go shower? I'll finish prepping everything."

I squeeze Luca once more. "I owe the elf man big time."

Chapter Twenty-One

JEMMA

Lukewarm water cascades down my soapy skin as Luca consumes my every thought. His kindness knows no bounds. His sexiness makes me ravenous. His banter is playful. He's the full glorious package. He makes me feel better, feel seen. Of all the men I could have slammed into, I ran into Luca. How did I get so lucky?

For real. How?

If I didn't know any better, I'd say it's a bit of Christmas magic. From scammed and alone to a perfect Parisian apartment complete with a French hottie, who, I might add, is currently waiting for me in a sexy Santa apron, ready and willing to bake Christmas cookies in honor of my mother.

Swoon.

I'm beyond grateful for everything my twisted bit of luck has brought me, but greedily, I want more.

I know I just met Luca, but it feels like we've known each other for years.

My time in Paris is limited, and I want to experience everything, including him. As daydreamy thoughts of Luca's sultry lips on mine fill my mind, a burst of icy cold water sputters from the showerhead, knocking me back to reality.

Shivering, I twist the knob and reach for my fluffy towel.

What if I'm getting ahead of myself? Luca's kindness could be just that—kindness. Nothing more.

Ugh!

I have a giant Eiffel Tower-sized problem—I want so much more.

Chapter Twenty-Two

JEMMA

Forty-five agonizingly long minutes have passed since I was in the same room as Luca. I can't get ready fast enough. My heart is racing in anticipation of our impromptu baking session.

Pushing aside any lingering doubts, I quickly finish getting ready, letting my hair fall more naturally today. I sift through the contents of my unpacked suitcase, finally selecting the perfect cream-colored sweater—the one that hugs me in all the right places. Before stepping out of the room, I dab my lips with a creamy pink gloss and brush some mascara over my eyelashes to ensure my blueish-green eyes pop.

Luca's back is turned to me when I enter the kitchen. Michael Bublé's "It's Beginning to Look a Lot Like Christmas" is playing through a small speaker resting on his dining table. One week ago, any Christmas song would make me cringe, but now my mouth is itching to sing along. I wait in the doorway, watching him move along the countertop humming along with the festive tune. My heart swells.

I snap a quick photo with my phone, capturing this perfect moment in time. I don't hesitate and quickly send it off to Gretchen, forgetting about the time difference again.

> Jemma: Looks like I'm staying at Luca's for the rest of my trip. He's a very thoughtful host. I'll tell you more later.

My eyes fall back to scanning every inch of Luca from behind. I can't find a single thing wrong with him. He's downright perfect. I let a tiny snicker escape, and Luca whips around.

"Is this music okay?" he asks, a hint of concern in his voice.

"It's perfect." I gleam. "I'm ready to get my bake on." I smirk, reaching for my cheeky Mrs. Claus apron perched next to the speaker.

"Whoa there, Santa's little helper." Luca chuckles, nudging a plate toward me with a perfectly golden pain au chocolat resting on it. "Eat first," he insists.

So damn perfect!

A playful grin simmers across his full lips. "I may have snuck out while you were in the shower to grab some pastries from the boulangerie around the corner. But when I got there, I panicked and realized I should have asked what you like. So, I also got a plain croissant too, if you'd rather."

I love how the word croissant rolls off his tongue—*kwuh-sahn.*

So fucking flawless!

"I will eat any pastry you put in front of me. I'm kind of spoiled when it comes to baked goods," I say, drawing the plate closer to me. "Gretchen's girlfriend is an incredible pastry chef"—I take a bite—"oh, but this is like nothing I've ever tasted before. Don't tell Suzy I said that." I giggle.

Luca laughs, his single dimple extremely present. "Your secret's safe with me."

I smile sweetly, gazing out the window and wishing for a bit of snow to fall to make this moment even more perfect.

"Coffee?" Luca asks, cutting in front of my view and nodding to the coffee machine.

"Always," I respond, falling in sync with the gorgeous man dressed in a Christmas apron and looking fine as hell.

I could definitely get used to this.

When I'm finished with one of the best pastries I've had in my entire life—not exaggerating—I slip over to the counter and attempt to ease into my apron, but the straps twist awkwardly in my hands.

"Allow me," Luca offers, stepping closer, his delicious scent happily invading my nose. He wraps the straps tightly around my waist, and then ties it around my neck, his fingers lingering just a moment too long.

Is that intentional? My heart does a little pitter patter.

We get to work, adding all the necessary ingredients to make a not-so-close-but-I-appreciate-the-attempt version of my mother's famous Christmas cookies. When Luca's back is turned, I add my mom's secret ingredient.

"Just a little sprinkle of love," I whisper to myself, adding an imaginary dash.

I know it sounds silly, but you can always tell when they're made with love, which is probably another reason why I haven't made them. I know they wouldn't have turned out. I swear dough can feel vibes, and I haven't been putting off good ones since I lost my mom. Making her favorite Christmas tradition without her didn't feel right until this moment. Being here in Luca's kitchen, pushing myself out of my boundaries and attempting to go with the flow feels right. I know my mom would agree. Plus, look at him in that apron. That sight alone would draw anyone back to the kitchen.

When it's time to roll the dough, I nudge him with my hip, smacking the rolling pin from his hand. "I need to do this step. My mother always said, 'Not too thin, not too thick.'"

I sprinkle a dusting of flour on my rolling pin, focusing intently as I roll out the dough, making it perfect. I lean in for a tree cookie cutter, feeling Luca's eyes on me. "What?" I whisper.

"You have a bit of flour—" he reaches out, his thumb gently swiping my cheek.

"Oh," I whisper, embarrassed, but eager for his touch.

"Got it," he says, letting his magnetic blue eyes linger on mine.

My breath catches in my throat.

Luca leans in and softly says into my ear, "I'm so glad you ran into me."

My skin tingles, practically vibrating. "Me too," I say, biting my bottom lip.

"There is something about you—something different. It's hard to describe."

I twist my mouth.

"No, it's a good thing. I know we just met, but I can't help but feel there's something bringing us together. Like a connection—pushing us. I don't know." He shakes his head. "Maybe I'm crazy."

"Maybe you're not." I bite my bottom lip, leaning into him, begging for him to take me.

Luca reaches around me, hooking his hand around my waist, closing the distance between us.

"But the cookies—"

"Can wait," he says, cutting me off with a sultry grin.

In one fluid motion, he lifts me effortlessly and places me onto the counter, positioning himself snugly between my thighs.

His eyes meet mine as if he's staring straight into my soul. "You've captured me, Jemma Jones. I've never met anyone like you before. Gosh, how do you have me feeling like this?"

I playfully shrug my shoulders, batting my eyelashes.

"J'ai envie de toi," he says, leaning in, his voice low and wanting, his breath hot on my skin.

My mind wanders to Colette as his hand travels along my inner thigh.

"Is this okay?" he asks.

Eh, fuck it! I nod slowly, quivering breathlessly. *I've never wanted anything more in my life.*

He cups my chin, pulling me closer until there's no space left for doubt. His delicate lips meet mine, kissing me gently at first, then more eagerly.

My hands instinctively weave through his hair, fingers tangling in the dark tousled strands—something I've craved since the very first moment we met.

His lips move to my neck, then to my ear, nibbling on the lobe as he whispers, "Should we take this to my bedroom?"

Biting my bottom lip, I nod. He scoops me off the counter and takes me into his room.

My eyes flutter open. I'm in Luca's bed. I must have fallen asleep.

The room is dark, but I know behind the blackout curtains, daylight is begging to break through. I'm certain it's still early in the day. The events of our morning unfold in my memories like a sweet dream.

Luca.

I stretch my hand across the bed, my fingers searching for him, but instead of finding him, my fingers brush against a note resting on his pillow.

The man loves leaving notes.

Naked, I wrap a blanket around myself and reach back for the crisp sheet of paper. Tossing my legs over the bedside, I tiptoe across the cold, wooden floor, the boards letting out soft moans as I move through the room. With a deep breath, I pull apart the heavy, velvety curtains, allowing the daylight to flood in, illuminating every corner. I hold the note up to read Luca's words.

> Jemma,
>
> I didn't want to wake you as you looked so peaceful. I had to step out for a bit. I promise we'll finish making the cookies when I get back.
>
> Luca

I can't help but feel a twinge of disappointment. What could be more important than lying in bed next to me, especially after the fiery moment we just shared? I anxiously tug at the blanket wrapped around me, wondering if I made a huge mistake.

Chapter Twenty-Three

JEMMA

He's up and gone before me again, just like the last four days. I always thought Parisians took their time—*joie de vivre* and all. I know he doesn't have to work, so where does he go? When I ask him about it, he simply says he has things to do. I don't press him because I know the French are private.

But come on, dude! You can't have "cookie time"—that's what I've been calling our little bedroom escapade—and then pretend our passionate moment never happened.

Ugh! Seriously, every time I think of it, I go red in the cheeks and get a bit lightheaded, but then the frustration creeps in, ruining it.

I feel like his roommate. His pal. Good ol' buddy Jemma, just hanging around. Sure, we see each other in passing, but there's no playful touching, no sweet kisses in the kitchen. Nothing!

So much for being perfect.

I have my own schedule, and he has his. But I'm not

going to let that stop me. I'm in Paris, and I've got a list to check off.

Seriously, I have a real handwritten list, from . . . you guessed it. Luca. On Monday morning, I woke to find a checklist of sights—for your blog—it read.

See, it's things like this that keep me wanting him. He can be thoughtful and attentive when the mood strikes. I still don't know about the whole blog idea, but the list has come in handy.

So far, I've toured the Louvre, Musée de l'Orangerie, and the Musée d'Orsay, with the d'Orsay being my favorite, especially the fifth floor with the Impressionists. I spent hours soaking in the works of Monet, Degas, and Renoir. One painting, *Bal du moulin de la Galette,* held me captive for what felt like an eternity, transporting me to another time.

Most days, it's been gloomy, with an afternoon shower. I've been hoping for snow, but it's yet to be seen. I wish it would snow before I leave. I'd love to see this magical city blanketed in white.

On another note, I'm quite proud of myself for mastering the metro system. I even got myself a reloadable Navigo pass with my photo and everything. I feel like a local when I pull it out and give it a swipe.

Plus, the metro is so much more efficient than the New York Subway system, and quite frankly, much cleaner. The downside is that it gets just as packed during rush hours, but I've figured out how to plan my days around that.

I'm also slightly obsessed with the Art Nouveau signs marking the Metro entrances. *Metropolitain.* They almost make you feel like you're going somewhere magical, but then you remember you're entering an underground transit system. At least they try. I was excited that my favorite museum even had an exhibition on the designs which made me appreciate them even more. The little things that bring me joy these days surprise me.

Have I said it enough? I. Love. Paris.

I've also seen the expansive views of the city from the steps of Sacré-Cœur, perused books at Shakespeare and Company, window shopped along the Champs-Élysées, walked along the dreamy Seine River, toured Notre-Dame, enjoyed an iconic hot chocolate from Les Deux Magots, and have eaten at more boulangeries than I can count on one hand. Don't judge. *When in Paris.*

But tonight, I'm veering from my list. I've done a bit of research on my own, and Luca will be accompanying me whether he likes it or not.

Chapter Twenty-Four

LUCA

"Where are you taking me?" I plead, following Jemma through the streets of *my* neighborhood. My darling little house guest has been very mysterious since demanding I join her for an unplanned outing this evening.

She crinkles her cute slender nose sprinkled with barely noticeable freckles—but of course, I noticed—and flashes me a playful grin.

"It's a surprise!" she chirps, yanking on my arm, tugging me down the busy sidewalk.

"I'm supposed to be showing you around Paris. Not the other way around. Are you sure you know where you're going?" I tease, knowing I'm about to get a rise out of her.

"Yes. I know exactly where I'm going." She turns to me with an exaggerated pout, her perfectly shaped eyebrows raised. "You're kind of a control freak, aren't you? You really need to chill and let me take the reins today." She impishly stomps her black-booted foot into the ground—

her *flat* black boot, that is. I think she's over heels, and with good reason. I'm not going to lie; I got off a bit teasing her about the cobblestones. I think it brought us closer together, though. And damn did those heels make her legs look great.

Focus.

She's staring at me, waiting for a response, and I can't help but chuckle.

"Luca!"

"Lead the way." I motion for her to continue. I'll give her credit; she's feisty, but there's a sweetness peeking out from behind her walls. I love the way she challenges me, like on the plane when she thought I had her seat. And when she thought I lied to her. I didn't lie to her about needing to be home, but I haven't been completely honest with her either.

I never expected to fall for her. This wasn't part of the plan. I only wanted to help her out of a bad situation.

Don't get me wrong—she's absolutely gorgeous, a little frustrating at first, but that's what drew me to her. Okay, hell—I'm a freaking liar—the moment I first laid eyes on her, I was taken by her. I never thought I'd see her again. But fate has a funny way of tossing things back at you, doesn't it?

When she called me that day, I knew I had to help her, but that was it. I would help Jemma find a place to stay and call it my good deed for the day, but once again, the universe had other plans for us. How was it possible that Paris, of all places, had zero availability? Well, it did have some vacancy, but there's no way in hell I was going to drop her off at one of the run-down hostels or seedy places my brother found for her. Jemma deserved better.

But still, I had no intention of falling for her.

I have too much on my plate right now. I should have been honest with her, but what's the point when she's leaving at the end of the month? We'll probably never see each other again.

"Almost there." She beams, her smile practically reaching her eyes.

When we cross the Seine, over the Pont Royal, I know exactly where she's leading us.

"Et voilà," Jemma announces, her blueish-green eyes sparkling triumphantly. It's so cute when she speaks French; she's much better at it than she realizes, especially when she stops overthinking it.

We're standing at the entrance to La Magie de Noël, the Christmas Market at the Jardin des Tuileries—my mother's favorite holiday tradition. My heart swells in my chest, feeling as if it might burst.

"I wanted to repay you for trying"—she makes little air quotes with her fingers—"to recreate a Christmas memory for me. Although, I think it's been replaced by a new one now." She bites her bottom lip and tugs on her braid.

It's something I've seen her do several times, and it tortures me. I want to grab her right here on the street and pull her close. I've never wanted anyone as badly as I want her right now. My mouth twitches, itching to kiss her.

I wish things didn't have to be so complicated. The other morning was a bit of a slip—a good slip—but I shouldn't let it happen again. It's not fair to her.

Maybe in another lifetime. If things didn't start off the way they did . . .

No matter what, I want to enjoy my time with her while it lasts. Does that make me a bad person?

Her features knit together, noticing my lack of reaction. "I hope this is okay?" she softly says, shrinking into herself.

"Oh, my goodness, yes. C'est parfait," I respond, flashing her a grateful smile. It's more than okay. It's perfect—she's perfect.

I don't deserve you.

"You really are one of a kind, Jemma with a J." Without thought, I grab her dainty hand, weaving my fingers through hers.

Her touch is electrifying. I'll miss this when she's gone. The thought of her leaving sends a shockwave through my body. I wish things were different, but we'll always have this moment. We'll always have Paris.

Her eyes sparkle with delight when we enter the market. I watch as her eyes bounce from one wooden chalet to another.

"It's like half-carnival, half-market?" she says, her gaze lingering on the towering Ferris wheel. "I see why this was your mother's favorite tradition. It's absolutely amazing."

"It really is the gem of Paris this time of year, but it can be a bit overwhelming, so let me take it from here," I offer, guiding Jemma toward a stall draped in garland.

I know this surprise is meant for me, but the need to take charge wells up within me. I want to ensure Jemma experiences everything this magical Christmas market has to offer. She's slowly finding her joy again, and this might just be the frosting on the cookie that makes it happen.

When we approach the stall, a friendly vendor asks, "How many?"

I flash him two fingers.

He ladles steaming red liquid from a copper cauldron into two tall cups and sprinkles a dash of nutmeg on top before exchanging them for a few euros.

Jemma shimmies next to me, rubbing her arm into mine. "Brrr," she murmurs.

"This will warm you up." I pass a cup to her, holding back the urge to wrap her in my arms. "No Christmas market can be enjoyed without first having a cup of vin chaud, hot mulled wine."

Jemma cups the drink in her hand, bringing it to her nose to inhale the fragrant blend of spices. Her face lights up before she takes a sip, and a smile breaks across her glossy lips. "Wow, c'est incroyable."

I flash her a satisfied smile. "Okay, now we're free to enjoy the rest of the market." I laugh.

With our warm cups in our hands, we begin to explore, weaving in and out of chalets, checking out each vendor. I know I said it before, but I love watching Jemma experience Paris. Each new sight sparks a light within her. I wish I could have spent time with her this past week, but I had other responsibilities that needed my attention.

"Be right back. You wait here," Jemma commands, dashing into an overflowing stall of handcrafted ornaments.

I do as I'm told. I watch as she thoughtfully plucks an item from a display, a pleased look settling across her face.

A few moments later, she returns. "For your tree." She grins, tucking a small package into her purse.

"Do I get to see it?" I question.

She shakes her head as her front teeth teasingly nibble on her bottom lip, slightly torturing me. "It's a surprise."

My eyes are busy trailing the outline of her mouth when she grabs my wrist and pulls me down the corridor. "Can we get one of those next?" Her gaze is now pointing directly at a ham raclette sandwich.

"Sure." I chuckle.

"Will you let me walk and eat it at the same time?" she says with a bit of sass as she dances around me. "Please, s'il te plaît," she taunts.

Gosh, she's cute.

"You're something else, Jemma." Another laugh escapes me. "This is one place I'll allow it." I wag my finger at her.

We already share inside jokes. Boy, am I screwed. I've let this go way too far.

I'm following Jemma, but before we can make it to the hut where the large wheel of melted cheese awaits, ready to be lavishly scooped onto sandwiches, Jemma comes to an abrupt halt.

She twirls around, her eyes lighting up like a kid on Christmas morning. "Oh, Luca. Regarde, c'est le Père Noël. Pouvons-nous prendre une photo?" Jemma bursts out in perfect French, a proud smile lighting up her beautiful features.

With a weary shake of my head, I surrender to Jemma. Seeing her this excited for a holiday she's written off and coming at me in perfect French, sends my heart into a flutter for more than one reason.

I let her drag me into the line to get our photo with Santa. Normally, I would find this silly, but for her, I'll do anything.

Things are becoming more complicated by the second. I need to be honest with her. But the truth could shatter everything. All the trust I've built could be gone in a flash.

I can't keep pretending. I need to be honest with her.

"Jemma, there's something I need to tell you," I muster the courage to say, my voice barely breaking through the noise of the crowd.

She doesn't hear me.

I clear my throat to start again, but the line shuffles forward.

"Jemma, there's something I want to tell you," I say again.

This time, she hears me. She whips around, her hair brushing against my face, and her blueish-green eyes clock onto mine, wide and questioning.

"Entrer," a lady calls out, motioning for us to step forward.

We step up and into the cozy wooden chalet adorned with over-the-top festive décor, where Santa sits regally in the center on a large chair. Jemma and I take our places beside him, ready for our photo.

Just as the photographer shouts, "Souriez," I spot *her* in the crowd.

My chest tightens.

She sees me too.

I'm not ready to deal with this right here, and especially not in front of Jemma. I need time to explain.

This can't be happening.

Her eyes are wildly trained on me, coming forth with rage.

The photographer snaps another photo.

My worlds are colliding. There's no stopping it now.

Colette is about to ruin everything.

Chapter Twenty-Five

JEMMA

Luca's face turns to stone as we step down from the chalet. I follow his gaze, and my stomach sinks.

My pulse quickens. This is it. I'm a homewrecker. Why did I sleep with him? I'm a horrible person.

I step back, leaning into the wooden hut, bracing for the worst. I'm about to cover my face when Colette comes in hot, screaming at Luca in rapid-fire French. There's no way I can keep up. The words roll fast and hot off her tongue. Luca interjects with his hands wildly flailing in the air.

Colette pauses, eyeing me up and down.

Luca takes a sharp breath. "Jemma." He pauses, and I wait for the words, *this is my girlfriend.*

I swallow hard, ready for my whirlwind romance with my French hottie to blow up at one of the most magical places in the world. I'm already planning my exit strategy, hoping they'll allow me enough time to pack in peace.

Her emerald eyes narrow as they dart over to me, making my stomach flip again.

"This is"—he hesitates, his expression souring"—Colette. My Sister."

Sister?

Did I hear him correctly? My brain crashes. There's no way I heard that correctly.

Colette, the stunning goddess of a woman, is his sister. HIS SISTER! My cheeks flame hot with embarrassment, turning the color of Santa's suit, giving away my foolishness.

Relief fills me.

I'm reaching my hand out to introduce myself when Luca announces, "I've got to go. I need air."

He storms away.

I'm rushing to keep up with him, my small legs unable to match his pace. Outside the market, I whip my head to the left and the right before finding Luca sitting on a bench with his head in his hands, his dark hair falling forward.

I drop down next to him, putting my hand on his shoulder. He's shaking, practically vibrating.

"Luca, are you alright?" I softly ask.

Luca slowly raises his head, tears filling his eyes. "My dad isn't well."

I gasp, covering my mouth. "Oh, Luca, I'm so sorry." I immediately feel awful for distracting him this month. Although, this does explain a lot of his behavior.

"What does that have to do with what just happened with your sister?"

Luca takes a deep breath, exhaling through his nose.

"When we met at the airport, I didn't lie to you, Jemma. I needed to be on that flight. I was supposed to stay in New York another week, but I got a call from Colette. She told me she made the decision to move my father into a memory care facility. She was taking him out of his home, the one he built with my mother—the only home he's known for decades. I was so angry. I booked the next flight to Paris, and that's when I ran into you."

I flash him a sympathetic nod, wanting him to continue.

"For years, Colette's been talking about it as my dad's condition progressed, but it wasn't time—not yet." The words get caught in his throat.

"Henri and I were against it from the beginning. We believed it would be better for him to stay at home as long as possible. I was even looking into hiring a full-time nurse to take care of him. But then Colette blindsided us. She waited until I was away for business. How could she do this?" He shakes his head.

"The worst part is that Colette doesn't even live here, but she's the one my dad left in charge of his healthcare. And then she moved to Italy with her husband and two children. So, I thought I could fight my dad's decision, but it turns out that since he made it when he was in his right mind, there was nothing Henri and I could do about it.

"She hasn't seen the good days; she only hears about the bad ones. I really thought we could reverse the damage with good doctors and memory games, but nothing worked. I knew this day would eventually come, but I didn't expect it to be now and like this.

"Colette has been trying to talk to me, to get me to understand her side of things, but I've been avoiding her. I just don't want to talk to her. She betrayed us—she betrayed my father."

"I'm so sorry Luca." I say softly.

He reaches for my hand. "It's okay. It's just going to take some time for everyone to adjust to our new normal."

"I can't imagine. I'm so sorry you're going through this."

A small smile percolates in the corner of his mouth, making his dimple pop. "I'm really glad you're here with me this Christmas." He gives my hand a quick squeeze. "You've been a bright light during a dark time."

"You know you could have told me." I tilt my head to rest on his shoulder.

"It's your vacation. I didn't want to burden you with my personal business."

I sit up straight, turning my knees to meet his, my cheeks prematurely blushing. "I think that line is a bit blurry already, don't you?"

"*Cookie time.*" He makes little air quotes, his blue eyes brightening.

A giggle bubbles up, and I respond, "Yes, that and the fact that I've met some of your family and shared stories about mine. You could have told me, Luca. I thought . . ."

His eyebrows raise slightly. "What?"

My head drops into my hand. "I thought—this is so silly now—but I thought Colette was your girlfriend." I raise my head to meet his gaze, unsure of what I'll find.

His mouth twists upward. "Je suis perplexe."

I huff. "The night you recused me—the night before —" I let my words trail. *The night before you had to move your father against your will.* "I noticed Colette kept calling you, and I thought maybe she was your girlfriend or something. Then she showed up the next morning after you left, and I was afraid to answer the door. She's intense. I was kind of scared of her."

I get a chuckle out of him. "You know you could have just asked me, right?"

"I didn't want to overstep. It was none of my business," I admit.

"Did you still think I had a girlfriend the day we"—he makes little air quotes again—"made cookies."

"No." I shrug my shoulders. "I don't know. I was pretty sure you didn't," I admit. "But then when I saw Colette coming in hot tonight, I wasn't so sure anymore. I was sure she was coming for me."

Luca shakes his head. "There's never a dull moment with you, is there?"

"Nope. I like to keep things interesting." I squish up my features. "Should we go back to the market?"

"I have a better idea," he says with a sexy wink.

Chapter Twenty-Six

JEMMA

"How big of a tree are we searching for?" I ask, navigating my way through Marché aux Fleurs, a floral shop that doubles as a Christmas tree store, nestled between the gorgeous Sainte-Chapelle and Notre-Dame.

This area is quickly climbing my list of favorite areas in the city. Just last night, we visited the Le Marché de Noël de Notre-Dame, another spectacular Christmas market, to make up for the night Colette ruined. Well, maybe not totally ruined. Let's just say it ended on a high note, if you catch my drift.

"I think we should get this one." Luca gestures toward a small tabletop tree.

I scrunch up my nose. "That's not a tree. It's a shrub."

"I take it that's a no," he replies, his gaze lingering on mine.

I bite my lip, feeling a familiar flutter in my stomach at the sight of him. Even in the most casual outfit—slim-cut dark blue jeans and a baby blue button-up poking out from under his dark jacket—he's perfect. Especially now that I know he's single and where he sneaks off to every morning.

For the first time, I notice a parade of longing glances directed at him, but he's completely oblivious; his eyes are glued to mine.

When I finally manage to peel my gaze away from him, I spy it—the tallest, most magnificent tree in the shop.

"This is the one!" I squeal as the earthy scent of fresh pine fills my senses. "This is the first tree I've bought in three years. It has to be absolutely perfect."

"Do you really think I can haul that giant thing all the way back to my apartment?" he asks, tapping his foot, brows raised.

"I guess I didn't think of how we'd get it home." I giggle, imagining us hauling my chosen tree back to Luca's apartment. "I do really love this tree, though." I pout, giving him my best puppy dog eyes.

"Oh, mon petit lapin," he says with a mischievous smirk, pulling me behind the towering evergreen, away from prying eyes. His lips crash into mine, igniting a burst of fireworks in my chest, my knees turning to jelly.

"But this tree . . ." I pull back, batting my eyelashes as I run my finger along the branches.

"I can't say no to you, can I?"

I shake my head dramatically, trying to hold back a smile, but failing miserably.

"Well, then you definitely can't say no to me when I ask you to be my date to my boss's Christmas party on Saturday."

"I would absolutely love to be your date. Well, as long

as this tree is really coming home with us." I dig into my bag and pull out a small wrapped package. I carefully remove the paper and delicately weave a branch through the loop. "It's ours now!" I declare, stepping back to admire the small oval-shaped glass ornament with a hand-painted elf on the front that I snagged at the Christmas market. "Now it's perfect."

The metro is packed, and it's not even rush hour.

Oops.

At least the shop attendant wrapped the tree in netting, making it a bit easier for Luca to transport.

"The things I do for you," Luca says with a twisted grin as he wrangles our perfect Christmas tree through the sliding doors.

With a few quick shuffles, the crowd parts just enough to give us a sliver of space to the right of the doors.

"It's just three stops," Luca keeps repeating under his breath. "Just three stops."

I yank my scarf up over my mouth, stifling a laugh that's bubbled up. Watching Luca with his arms wrapped around our gigantic tree is downright hilarious. This is something I'll never forget.

We jostle with the car as a panorama of blurry, fast-moving tunnels flash by, and before we know it, an announcement signals our stop. Luca lets out a loud sigh of relief.

"That wasn't so bad now, was it?" I joke.

"That's easy for you to say," Luca playfully responds.

A wave of gasps echo through the people behind us as we exit the train car. On the platform, Luca hoists the tree over his shoulder and carries it up the steps and the rest of the way to his apartment.

I follow closely behind, snapping photos of our adventure along the way and sending them off to Gretchen.

Jemma: I think I've found THE ONE!

Gretchen: The tree or the man?

Jemma: Both!

Gretchen: First, cookies and now this. Jemma Jones is back!

Jemma: I don't want to leave! I'm falling hard for Luca!

Gretchen: Just enjoy your time together. Everything will fall into place.

Gretchen: Trust me! 😉

Chapter Twenty-Seven

JEMMA

Once again, I'm in spiky heels standing on a cobblestone sidewalk. But this time, it's completely warranted. Gretchen's Christmas-red A-line dress demands the perfect footwear. It would be a crime to pair it with anything less than the perfect shoe.

I feel amazing in this dress. I love the way the lace bodice hugs my figure, while the tulle skirt billows around me. I can't help but feel like a princess, and I have my Prince Charming linked around my arm to prove it.

But not even the confidence this dress is feeding me could prepare me for the building I'm staring at.

"Is this your boss's home?" I ask, my eyes traveling upward, feeling small and insignificant, yet completely enamored by the sight. I've seen some stunning buildings in Paris, but this one takes the whole darn cake.

The creamy stone structure appears to be a recently renovated Haussmann-style building tucked near the edge of the seventh. The second floor is elegantly defined by one long continuous terrace, while the next two levels showcase charming wrought-iron Juliet balconies with intricate designs. But the true gem is the top floor with its expansive wrap-around balcony that follows the curve of the building, beneath a mansard roof with dormer windows breaking through the steep slopes. I could stare at this building for hours. It's architecture porn.

"His is the top floor in case you were wondering." Luca leans in, whispering in my ear.

My jaw drops. "The entire floor?" I stammer, counting the number of windows that make up his boss's home.

Nine. There are nine street-facing windows. Luca has four, and I thought his place was large for Paris.

"Maybe now would be a good time to tell me more about your job."

Luca chuckles as a doorman drags a towering glass entryway door back for us. Which is clearly not the original, I might add.

"Bonsoir, Monsieur Dubois." The man nods to Luca as we pass.

We cross through a grand common area with beautifully designed marble floors. A sweeping staircase calls to us from the left, but we choose the path leading toward three long, narrow marble steps and up to a tiny glass lift. The black metal cage is intricately detailed with rosettes and vines.

Luca calls for the elevator as I shift nervously while we wait. I'm meeting his co-workers for the first time, and I want to make a good impression on the people Luca spends his time with.

He takes my trembling hand in his, calming my racing nerves.

"I think I was less nervous about meeting your family," I admit.

"Don't worry; everyone will love you."

With my free hand, I nervously press down the fabric that's billowing out from under my jacket.

"You're fidgeting." Luca grins, squeezing my hand.

"Oh," I respond, letting my gaze drop to the stone flooring.

"You look absolutely stunning tonight," Luca says, drawing my attention back to him.

A rush of warmth floods my cheeks as he leans in, brushing his lips softly against my cheek in a gentle kiss. He pulls back just as the lift arrives. We step inside the metal cage, and the door glides shut. Luca presses a button, and with a playful twist of his body, he reaches for me, pulling me against his chest. He leans in, capturing my lips with a tender kiss that sends me spinning. I could get used to this life. I never want this trip to end.

Inside the lavish apartment, someone greets us at the door and offers to take our coats. Luca helps me out of mine and hands it to a woman who disappears behind a double glass doorway.

Luca takes my hand and leads me into a circular room —the curved part of the building I saw from the street. Massive floor-to-ceiling windows wrap around every wall, offering amazing views of cathedrals and domes in the distance. I search for the Eiffel Tower, but I don't see it. Such a shame to have everything else in view but that.

In the center of the room, people are chatting in large groups and sipping on sparkling beverages. Luca approaches one of the gatherings and introduces me to a few of his co-workers. They don't seem interested in me, and I try not to take it personally. Instead, I sink into Luca, letting his arm wrap around me. This is all I need, but Luca catches me off guard, as his eyes nervously dart around the room.

"Will you excuse me for a moment?" he says, kissing the top of my forehead.

I open my mouth to plead for him to stay and not leave me alone with these unfriendly people, but I don't have a chance. He's already out of my sight.

I sigh, lingering on the outskirts of the group.

I catch a rail-thin woman with a turned-up nose and a sleek bob eyeing me. Her mouth contorts with disgust as she turns to the gentleman next to her and says very loudly, "Peux-tu croire qu'elle porte cette horrible robe?"

The man snickers as his eyes slowly trail the entire length of my body.

"Pouah," she puffs. "Je mourrais avant de porter ça!"

The whole group bursts into laughter.

My heart pounds in my chest as my mind races to catch up.

They're making fun of my dress.

The woman turns to take a drag of the slim cigarette resting between her fingers.

I hope that thing kills you.

Harsh, Jemma. That's not like you.

Okay, maybe not kill you, but make you sound like a

man and give you premature wrinkles. That's right; take that, karma. Screw these people.

"Je parle français." I force a cocky smile and push my way through the group, desperate to find Luca.

I dart into the next room, my heart still pounding with adrenaline. I shrink as far back into the corner as I possibly can, hoping to blend in while I wait for Luca to return, but I know that's impossible.

Glancing down at my dress, I still feel a flicker of love for it, but it quickly fades as I check out the women in the room with their effortlessly chic pantsuits and sophisticated floor-length dresses. My red frilly dress stands out like a sore thumb. When Luca said Christmas party, I assumed reds and greens, but boy was I wrong. Maybe that evil woman did have the right to mock me. I wish Luca had been there to defend my honor.

Where the hell is he?

My eyes scan the room, but still, there's no sign of Luca. Where is my prince when this princess needs rescuing?

As I tug on the fabric of my not-so-incognito gown, a waiter strolls by with a full tray of champagne, and I quickly grab one of the flutes from the tray. The beverage may not make me invisible, but hopefully it will quell the rising tide of embarrassment.

"Luca's a great guy, isn't he?" A gruff voice rumbles from next to me, catching me mid-sip.

I turn, swallowing, before replying, "Yes, he really is. One of the best." I smile, hoping he's not here to poke fun at me too.

"I overheard you're American, but I didn't catch your name, dear?" The man is older, with a thick mustache framing his full upper lip.

"It's Jemma," I say, extending one hand and keeping my other tightly curled around the narrow stem of my glass.

"Alain," he introduces himself, taking my hand and flipping it over to kiss the top of it, his lips feeling sloppy against my delicate skin. "Luca's boss," he adds.

Just great.

I manage an awkward smile, retracting my hand as quickly as I can. I'm dying to wipe his slobber off my skin, but I'm most certainly not going to do it on Gretchen's dress. Even if it's not appropriate for this party, I still love it. So, I uncomfortably let my hand air dry, shaking it lightly behind me.

Yuck.

"Luca is one of my best employees," Alain continues, his voice swelling with pride. "He's been with me for ten years. I don't know what I'd do without him. He's one of the best in the business."

I nod, a small smile creeping onto my lips. It's nice to hear of his fondness for Luca.

"Are you here on holiday?" Alain's beady eyes glint with curiosity, taking more of an interest in me than his employees.

"Yes, but I leave soon." I frown, taking a sip of my bubbly champagne.

"Paris is dreamy this time of year, isn't it?" He leans in closer, a wink punctuating his comment.

"It is lovely," I reply. "I wish I didn't have to go back to New York so soon."

"What do you do for work back in the States?" he asks.

"I'm in advertising analysis for Foster & Sons," I say, the words rolling off my tongue out of habit. "I mean, I was—" My voice trails off as I struggle to find the words to continue. *It's complicated.*

Alain tilts his head thoughtfully. "Oh, is that how you met Luca?"

"Pardon?"

"Yes, that must be how the two of you met. Foster & Son's was one of Luca's consulting projects while he was in New York."

Confusion wraps around me.

When I don't respond, the husky man continues, "My company is one of the most sought-after in the world when it comes to getting businesses back on track before the new year, and Luca is the best at trimming the fat."

I stare at him, the ground feeling unsteady. "I'm the fat he trimmed," I say through gritted teeth.

Heat surges to my cheeks as the party around me spins into a blur.

An embarrassed expression crosses Alain's pudgy face. "I just assumed when you said you worked for Foster & Sons that's how you and Luca met."

"No, I met Luca at the airport."

None of this makes sense, but then suddenly everything clicks into place. Luca was the one sitting at the end of the table in the conference room—the one Tyler had been staring at—the one urging Tyler to say the words they rehearsed together.

My stomach lurches.

"Luca lied to me," I say under my breath.

He knew who I was from the moment we ran into each other at the airport. He knew who I was when he offered his place to stay. He was trying to clear his conscience. Were all those nice things he did for me all a ruse? But why?

I take a shaky sip of my champagne, the bubbles prickling my lips. "Please excuse me. I need to leave."

Alain's mustached lip forms an incredulous O-shape. He stands frozen as I rush past him.

Desperate to get out of this apartment as fast as I can, I weave in and out of rooms, searching for my coat, when I spot Luca talking to a woman with high cheekbones and pouty lips.

My vision blurs as tears spill over and race down my cheeks. Everything about this party was a bad idea.

When Luca catches my glare, my chest tightens. *Liar* is all I can think when I see him.

"Jemma?" he questions, reaching toward me.

I recoil, stepping back. "No."

"What's wrong?" he presses.

When I don't respond, Luca's expression quickly shifts from confusion to hurt.

"I'm leaving, Luca." I slip past him, rushing toward the door.

"Wait, Jemma. Don't go!" he calls after me. "Let me go with you." He's quick on my heels, following me into the hallway.

"No, I'm leaving Paris!" I shout, pressing the round button on the wall over and over, anxiously summoning the elevator, feeling trapped.

"Leaving Paris, but why?" A stunned look falls over his face, his features freezing in place.

The elevator dings, and I step inside, the door positioned to close.

"Because you lied to me," I manage to say before the door seals shut, the sound of his voice fading into the silence just as my heart plummets to my feet.

Chapter Twenty-Eight

LUCA

I knew who she was—Jemma with a J.

I first saw her in the conference room at Foster & Sons. She was just a name to me. Until she wasn't.

I've done this thousands of times—coaching people on what to say and evaluating them afterward to help them improve on the process going forward.

I never let myself get attached. It's part of the reason I love international projects. I know I'll never see these people again.

But I did. I saw her again.

And again.

And again.

And again.

I couldn't ignore her. She was everywhere.

I didn't want to admit this, but I overheard her and her co-worker, who I later found out was her best friend, talking in the hallway after she was let go. I heard the speech Gretchen gave Jemma about finding herself.

My heart broke for her, and in that intense moment, I found myself reevaluating whether this job was truly right for me. I was the axeman who ruined people's lives. I came in and chopped up companies for the sake of filling the pockets of greedy CEOs and shareholders. I'd move quickly, leaving before I could fully grasp the devastation I was causing. I never had to face the people I hurt.

But then she slammed into me at the airport.

At first, I didn't know it was her. She didn't have her hair in that cute little side braid that I've come to adore. No, she had her honey-blonde hair down, flowing freely around her beautiful face. It wasn't until our eyes locked that I felt something familiar about her. And then, *bam*, it hit me when I looked down at her boarding pass. Jemma with a J. The girl in the conference room. Foster & Sons.

In that moment, I was nervous and had to get away. I couldn't have her recognize me and cause a scene. Plus, I was in a hurry. But quickly, it became apparent she had no clue who I was, so it was easy to escape, thinking I'd never see her again, even if part of me wished I would.

Then we crossed paths again. How does that happen?

Fate. That's how it happens. Like I was being taunted by the universe. I knew I had to make things right, or at least I had to try. I didn't want to admit that I knew her, especially while confined in such a small space with hundreds of witnesses. I knew Jemma wouldn't take it well. She's feisty like that. So, after the whole seat debacle—which, I might add, could have gone a little better on my part, but I really did need to be on that flight. The next morning, I was moving my dad into his care facility. I still can't believe my sister had the audacity to orchestrate this whole charade while I was out of the country.

Actually, scratch that, I can. Colette has always been a bit conniving.

So, when I saw Jemma heading to the long restroom queue, I sprang into action, quickly coming up behind her. I startled her—it was cute. She wasn't expecting me.

"Oh, it's you," she said with such bitterness, but I could sense there was a spark of affection behind her words. The way her eyes traced my face, the way she stood, shifting with slight uncertainty—I knew I felt something between us.

When our flight was over, I was sad to see her go, filing down the narrow aisle, drifting into a sea of travelers.

So never in a million and one years did I think she'd track me down.

When I answered the phone from an unknown number—which I never do, especially when I'm off the clock—I was shocked to hear her voice.

But how? How could Jemma be calling me?

We never exchanged numbers, but somehow when we collided, she ended up with some of my paperwork.

So, when I heard her trembling voice through the phone, I knew I had to help her. I couldn't ignore this calling, and after hearing her conversation with Gretchen, I couldn't let her go back to New York with no job and no perfect Paris vacation.

I wanted to help her. I *had* to help her.

Sure, things started off with less-than-ideal circumstances—that whole I'm the whole reason you don't have a job thing. But it led me to her.

It led me to—

"Jemma," I shout, losing my train of thoughts as I burst down the last flight of stairs, catching sight of the portier pulling the door back for her.

I was sure I'd beat her to the ground level, but I was wrong.

My dress shoes slide across the polished stone floor as I race to catch up. "Jemma!" I plead, desperation taking over my voice, but she slips through the towering glass doors without giving me a glance, her blonde hair flapping in the wind behind her.

"Tiens la porte!" I shout.

The portier dutifully holds the door, the winter wind striking my face as I burst out of the building.

Frantically, my eyes scan the street for her slim silhouette. My heart lurches when I spot her crossing the road.

I can't let her leave. I need to explain.

"Wait!" I shout, taking off in her direction.

She quickens her pace, walking much too fast for someone in heels, but that's when I notice her black slingback pumps dangling from her dainty fingers.

No shoes and no coat. The poor girl must be shivering.

I need to make this right, but Jemma turns toward the Seine.

"You're going the wrong way," I shout, breaking into a light jog, coming up behind her.

Jemma halts in her tracks when she practically runs into a blue and white taxi sign.

She turns to me, pain flickering in her eyes. "You were there that day. At Foster & Sons."

I step closer, my pulse racing, knowing I need to tread lightly, or I'll lose her forever.

"You were in that meeting when I got fired. Admit it."

"I was."

"Why didn't you tell me?" Her voice trembles.

"I wanted to. I was eventually—"

"When?" she cuts me off, shaking her head, her golden locks whipping around her face. "I knew this was too good to be true—that *you* were too good to be true. This isn't some cheesy movie where everything works out perfectly in the end. This is real life, where I find out the guy I've been falling for is a complete and total liar."

The pain in her voice pierces through me, and I reach out, desperate to be close to her. But she steps back just as a taxi pulls up, idling beside us.

"Please. Let me explain."

She climbs into the back seat, her eyes shimmering with unshed tears as she stares at me from the window.

"Jemma," I call out, my voice choking on regret. "I'm sorry."

But it's too late.

The taxi pulls away, taking Jemma and a piece of my heart with it.

Chapter Twenty-Nine

JEMMA

In the cab, I burst into tears.

I'm embarrassed. I feel betrayed. The pain in my chest won't stop aching.

I've told him things—personal things I haven't told anyone. I swallow down the lump that's restricting my throat.

None of this was real. Everything was a lie. I knew this was too good to be true. This is real life, not some silly rom-com where everything works out perfectly in the end. I can get over him keeping his family issues from me, but this is a whole new level of fucked up.

I need my best friend right now—I need Gretchen. She'll know what to say. She'll help me make sense of this whole thing.

I slide my phone from my black clutch resting on my lap. With shaking hands, I text the one person I trust most in the world, praying for a quick response.

Jemma: I need you! NOW!!!

Gretchen: I'm walking to the subway RN. What's going on?

Jemma: You're not going to believe this . . .

Gretchen: Type faster. You're worrying me.

Jemma: Luca works for the company Foster & Sons hired to fire me. He's a hatchet man, Gretch! He's known who I am this entire time!!!!!!!! 💔

Gretchen: OMG. How is that even possible?

Gretchen: Where are you right now?

Jemma: I'm in a cab heading back to Luca's apartment. I left him on the street. He was trying to explain himself. I couldn't listen. I had to leave. I'm going to pack. Then I'm taking a cab to the airport. I don't care if I have to sleep there until I can get a flight home. I just can't be here with him. He's a big, fat liar.

I'm waiting for Gretchen's response when my phone starts vibrating in my already shaking hand. I quickly accept the call, yanking the phone toward my ear. The cabbie stares at me with curious eyes in the rearview mirror.

"Gretchen!" I exclaim, tears erupting from me like a

volcano.

"You're not going to the airport!" she demands.

My jaw drops. "Of course I am. He lied to me."

A burst of laughter echoes through my phone.

"Hello, Gretch?"

More laughter.

My heart sinks. "Are you really laughing right now?"

"Yes! This is the best thing I've ever heard."

"What's wrong with you? He knew who I was, Gretchen! The whole time!"

"He's the reason you're in Paris. Don't you see that? Luca is the one who set you on this path to finding yourself, even if he didn't know it. Nothing is accidental. Divine fate is always working its magic."

"You sound a little too woo-woo for me right now. I just need you to tell me I'm not crazy. And it's okay for me to go home. I tried. I really did."

Muffled sounds roar into my ear as a sharp screech pulsates through the phone. I immediately recognize the familiar sounds of the subway. I should be home with Gretchen. Not here on this silly trip.

"I can't do that," she says sternly.

My breath gets caught in my throat.

"Jemma, I need you to take a few deep breaths and listen. Okay."

I nod, even though she can't see me.

She continues, "Everything that happened the day you got let go from Foster & Sons led you to Paris. And to him. Didn't you say you ran into him at the airport? Like, literally ran into the very man that caused you to lose your job

—the very gorgeous man that set this whole thing into motion. If that's not fate, I don't know what is."

My mind drifts to the elf man, the seat fiasco, and the paper in my carry-on. It seems too serendipitous to be real. This kind of stuff happens in the movies. Not real life.

Gretchen clears her throat. "Are you still there?"

"Yes, I'm still here," I whimper.

"I didn't mean to laugh, but I can't help but think that this is exactly what was supposed to happen. I told you everything happens for a reason. This was all part of a bigger plan. He picked your faceless name from an employee list, right?

"Uh huh."

"You can't be mad at him for doing his job," she says.

"But when we collided into each other at the airport, he called me *Jemma with a J* as he handed my ticket back to me. He knew who I was at that very moment. I thought he was being rude, but he was putting the pieces together. He recognized the name and then me. He was in the conference room, Gretchen. He was there. Then somehow, he was in my seat. On the plane. He was everywhere."

"Fate," she interrupts.

"Whatever it is, it was cruel. It all makes sense now. He felt bad, so he was trying to play Mr. Nice Guy."

"And then you got scammed," she reminds me. "And who came to your rescue?"

"I only called him because I found his phone number on a piece of paper from when we collided. He was the only person I knew here."

"Fate!" She's practically screaming the word at me. "Can't you believe just for a minute that he liked you, and that's why he offered his place to stay? I doubt he would have done that for Sally if she were the one he had run into."

I huff, slinking further into my seat.

"Jemma, you've been sending me photos all week. I've never seen you so happy. You seemed like your old self again." She clears her throat. "Correction, you're better than your old self. A new Jemma."

"But he lied, Gretchen." I sniffle. "How can I get over that?"

The cab yanks to the right, coming to a stop. I pass the driver my card with tears streaming down my cheeks.

"Luca brought something out in you, Jem. This trip would never have happened if he hadn't set things in motion. I think this is the most romantic story I've ever heard."

The driver passes me my card, and as I'm tucking it into my wallet, he swings the door open for me. "For what it's worth, I believe in second chances," the driver says, with sympathy coating his vibrant teal eyes. "Plus, it sounds like someone up there wants you together." A small smile tugs at the corner of his lips as he tilts his head back, eyes tracing an invisible line to the clouds.

I nod, offering a half-grin.

"See? Even that guy knows it, Jemma," Gretchen says, pulling me back to our conversation. "So, what are you going to do?" she presses.

"I don't know. Everything is an absolute mess," I

respond. "He's a liar. I wish he could understand how much he hurt me. I trusted him."

"Jemma, I'm so sorry."

My body tightens. The words I hear don't belong to the lecturing voice coming through the phone. I shift on my feet in one quick motion, spinning around, my tulle skirt flapping in the wintery breeze.

"Is that Luca?" Gretchen shouts in my ear.

The gorgeous specimen of a man who first caught my attention at the airport is standing on the sidewalk, tears building in his frosty blue eyes, making them shimmer under the night sky. He takes a shy step forward, arm reaching toward me.

I pull back, unsure.

"I didn't expect to fall in love." The words fall softly from his mouth.

My hand with my phone drops heavy to my side, weighing like an anchor, tethering me to his revelation.

"Y-you love me?" I stammer, my emotions whirling.

"Of course I do. I know I should have told you everything from the start. I wanted to. I really did, but things got out of hand. There was never a good time. I was falling for you hard and knew if I told you, you'd react—well, like this." He softly chuckles. "I know it's no excuse, but everything with my dad and my sister had my head all out of sorts. But one thing I do know is that I love you, Jemma Jones."

"She loves you too." I hear Gretchen screeching from the device that's gripped tightly in my right hand.

I drag the phone back to my mouth. "I'm going to have

to call you back, Gretch." I don't wait for a response before hanging up and slipping my phone into my purse.

"So, you love me?" I taunt.

A wide grin cracks over Luca's stupidly handsome face. "You know I do."

"But you lied to me," my voice wobbles.

He takes a step closer, reaching for my hands. He clutches them tightly. "I can never regret what I did because it brought us together, but I'll spend forever making it up to you if that's what it takes." He pulls me tight against his chest. "I've waited my whole life to find you, Jemma. You're my person, and I think the universe knew that. We were bound to find each other one way or another. You can't deny that."

Hot tears roll down my cold cheeks.

Luca reaches up, runs his finger under my eye, wiping them away. "I never meant to hurt you. You must believe that."

I study his frosty blue eyes, the eyes that captured me the moment we met. He's telling the truth.

"I love you, Jemma with a J," he whispers into my ear, his breath warm against my skin. "I love how brave, funny, and smart you are. I love that you fidget when you're nervous. I love how stubborn you can be. I love everything about you."

A joyful smile breaks across my face, sending a warmth to my heart. "Je t'aime aussi, Luca. I love you too."

Chapter Thirty

JEMMA

"It's finally snowing," I exclaim, twirling around Luca as we stroll along the Seine, the Eiffel Tower emerging as a frosted silhouette against the dusky sky.

"It's a rare Christmas miracle." Luca smirks. "I haven't seen a white Christmas in"—he rubs his chin, his eyes drawn to the sky—"gosh, fifteen years."

"That's crazy. It's not Christmas without snow," I respond, a fluffy snowflake landing on my cheek.

Paris feels alive in this moment, as if it's a real being with a heart, beating with happy souls experiencing this Christmas magic as one.

Luca takes my hand in his, leading me toward the edge of the river, positioning us perfectly to face the snow-dusted tower. Facing forward, he wraps his arms around me, drawing me into his chest. I can't control the smile stretching along my face. This has been the best Christmas I've had since I lost my mom.

"You know, my dad loved you." Luca leans forward, pressing a soft kiss on my cheek.

This morning, Luca took me to meet his father. The visit started off wonderfully, and at first, I thought Luca had every right to be mad at his sister. His father was funny and charming, just like his son, but as the morning progressed, so did signs of his illness. It was hard watching someone shift like that. I know Luca's heart breaks each time that happens, but he's in a good facility, and he'll get the care he needs. The wounds his sister caused will take time to heal, but Colette did the right thing.

After that, the rest of the family gathered at Henri and Mia's for a feast fit for royalty. Colette stopped by with her family, and it was lovely to finally officially meet her. I even told her the story of how I thought she was Luca's girl-friend—I swear the woman didn't stop laughing for ten straight minutes.

Then, I video chatted with my dad. We reminisced about my mom—something we've avoided for a long time. Or maybe my dad always wanted to, but I skirted around it. Either way, it felt good, like we were keeping her memory alive. I promised to come see him when I get back, and this time, I mean it.

"My phone's buzzing." I pull away from Luca, my hand sliding into my purse.

A photo of Gretchen and Suzy with wide smiles lights up my screen.

Gretchen: Santa was really good to me this year . . .

Pinching the screen, I zoom in. Gretchen's hand is splayed out with a striking diamond wrapped around her ring finger.

> Gretchen: I said yes!! Getting married next Christmas!

I bounce up and down, happy tears coating my eyes. "Suzy proposed!" I flash the photo at Luca.

"Tell the happy couple congratulations," Luca says.

> Jemma: Luca and I both congratulate you! This is the best news ever!!! I can't wait to hear all about it! You deserve all the happiness in the world. Love you both!

"Today is absolutely perfect," I say, falling back into the comfort of Luca's arms.

He squeezes me tight and kisses the top of my head. "It's almost time," Luca whispers.

My eyes are trained on the tower, waiting for it to erupt into the sparkling icon that I've fallen in love with, when I hear a man's voice coming from beside us. "Would you like me to take your photo? It's a stunning backdrop for such a beautiful couple."

"That would be wonderful. Merci beaucoup." Luca reaches into his jacket for his phone and passes it to the man standing next to us.

When my eyes reach the man, my jaw drops. I nudge Luca. "It's him."

Luca flashes me a puzzled grin, his eyebrow cocked.

"The elf man," I whisper into his ear as we shift around for our photo, positioning the Eiffel Tower and the Seine behind us.

Luca shakes his head. "C'est impossible."

"So was us running into each other over and over again," I remind him.

"Smile," the man calls out as the tower behind us bursts into a radiant golden glow, reflecting like stars in the man's already sparkling eyes.

When he hands the phone back, Luca and I stare at the image. Goosebumps prickle my skin, and my mouth drops.

Behind us in the photo is a man wearing a tattered red Santa hat. My heart races. Could it really be the same guy from New York? What are the odds?

My gaze drifts over my shoulder.

He's gone.

"What?" Luca questions, curiosity lighting up his blue eyes as he stares past me.

I let a soft chuckle release. "Nothing."

That's a story I'll save for another time.

Luca smiles, his dimple flaring as his fingers gently cradle my chin, drawing my mouth toward his. When our lips finally meet, the entire world around us fades away. Pulling back, his fingers brush my cheek as he tucks my hair behind my ear.

For the millionth time, I wonder, how did I get so lucky? It turns out that losing my job and getting scammed was the best thing that could have happened to me. But how can we make this work? I live in New York, and Luca lives in Paris.

Tears prick my eyes as Luca wraps me in his arms, drawing me closer. I sink into his warmth, leaning my head against his chest, hearing his heart beat—for me.

"I can't believe I leave in the morning." My chest aches as the words leave my mouth. "I don't want this vacation to end. I love you, Luca."

"Stay," he whispers.

Epilogue
LUCA

SIX MONTHS LATER

"That was the day I asked you to stay," I say, catching Jemma eyeing the photo on my mantle—the one of us from Christmas last year.

"You framed it," she squeals.

"Of course. It was the first thing I did when you left," I reply, crossing the room to meet her.

"Aww," she coos, a soft smile dancing along her lips.

Jemma left shortly after the new year, so she could pack up her apartment, visit her dad, and apply for her long-stay visa. We're still working out all the details, so we can ensure she'll be here for the long haul, but I've got things covered. I reach into the pocket of my jacket, feeling the unmistakable shape of a ring pressing against the fabric.

When you know, you know—right?

"I'm so excited to finally be back," she declares, twirling over to the window, the sunlight catching her honey blonde hair. "I've missed this place so much. It's a shame we have to move." She pouts.

Oh, remember that woman I was talking to at my boss's Christmas party right before Jemma stormed in? Well, she's the head of human resources. I was asking her about taking a sabbatical. After everything that happened with Jemma and Foster & Sons, I knew I couldn't do my job anymore. Which also means, this apartment is unaffordable now. But honestly, that's okay.

Jemma and I can find something that feels right for us —something to mark the start of our life together.

You won't believe this, but her first blog post exploded into something beyond our wildest expectations. Instead of the travel blog I was encouraging, she wrote about us. It spiraled into a book deal, and *Just My Merry Luck* is set to come out next Christmas.

Fate is sneaky, isn't it?

Everything truly does happen for a reason.

The End

Acknowledgments

First, I must start by thanking my incredibly encouraging husband, Jeremy. Your constant support makes it possible for me to chase my dreams. I'm so glad I get to experience life alongside you. Our trip to Paris forever changed me, and I will always cherish our unforgettable memories and the inside jokes we created from that amazing trip.

I would also like to thank my writing community. To EJ Gore, your encouragement has been priceless. Stacey Spangler, our chats and check-ins have been what I needed to stay focused. And to the wonderful authors I've connected with on Instagram—Hayley Anderton, Bethany Russo and Jessica Huntley, just to name a few.

To my family, thank you for being my biggest cheerleaders. If you ever meet one of my parents, I'm sure they'll tell you about my books.

I'm immensely grateful to my editor, Nichole Heydenburg, at Poisoned Ink Press. You're a dream to work with, and your feedback has helped me grow as a writer.

To Emily for being the last set of eyes on this book.

A special thank you to Miblart for designing the perfect cover for this story.

Lastly, to you, my readers—whether this is your first

Jamie Lee Fry book or you've been following my journey from the beginning, I'm forever grateful for your support.

Subscribe

Join my mailing list and become a part of my exclusive community of readers. By subscribing to my monthly author newsletter, you'll get a sneak peek of my upcoming projects and be the first to know about book releases, cover reveals, and even ARC opportunities. You'll also get access to exclusive content, special offers, and behind-the-scenes insights into my writing process. Don't miss this unique opportunity to connect with me and be a part of my journey as an author.
https://www.authorjamieleefry.com

Jamie Lee Fry is the award-winning author of The Bloodline Curse, the first book in the Dark Magic Series. Her work spans multiple genres, including psychological thrillers, young adult fantasy, and festive sweet romance.

When she's not busy plotting her next novel, Jamie enjoys hiking, stand-up paddleboarding, cross-country skiing, traveling, and consuming questionable amounts of coffee.

She currently resides in Bend, Oregon, with her husband, Jeremy, and their two furry companions, Zaria and Dexter.

Connect with Jamie:
Instagram: @author_jamieleefry
Author Website: www.authorjamieleefry.com

www.ingramcontent.com/pod-product-compliance
Lightning Source LLC
Chambersburg PA
CBHW032300310726

48973CB00008B/2471